A F T E R

T H I S   N I G H T

Book #2 in the Seductive Nights series

Lauren Blakely

ALSO BY LAUREN BLAKELY
Available at all fine e-tailers

ALSO BY LAUREN BLAKELY
Available at all fine e-tailers

ABOUT
AFTER THIS NIGHT

"Let me control your pleasure."

Their world was passion, pleasure and secrets.

Far too many secrets. But Clay Nichols can't get Julia Bell out of his mind. He's so drawn to her, and to the nights they shared, that he can't focus on work or business. Only her. And she's pissing him off with her hot and cold act. She has her reasons though–she's trying to stay one step ahead of the trouble that's been chasing her for months now, thanks to the criminal world her ex dragged her into. If only she can get out of this mess, then maybe she can invite the man who ignites her back in her life, so she can have him– heart, mind and body.

He won't take less than all of her, and the full truth too. When he runs into her again at her sister's wedding, they have a second chance but she'll have to let him all the way in. And they'll learn just how much more there is to the intense sexual chemistry they share, and whether love can carry them well past the danger of her past and into a new future, after this night...

The sequel to the sensual, emotionally-charged erotic romance, Night After Night, from the New York Times and USA Today Bestselling author Lauren Blakely...

This book is dedicated to Gale, who listens to my stories, and helps shape them. You are indispensable to me, and I am so glad our paths crossed.

CHAPTER ONE

The dress was so perfect it brought a tear to her eye.

"He's going to have the breath knocked out of him when he sees you walking down the aisle," Julia managed to say while wiping her hand across her cheek.

Her sister, McKenna, twirled once in front of the three-way mirror at Cara's Bridal Boutique deep in the heart of Noe Valley, admiring the tea-length dress she'd picked for her wedding in a few weeks. The dress was pure McKenna, down to the flouncy taffeta petticoat underneath the satin skirt.

"It's so playful and pretty at the same time," Julia said.

"Speaking of pretty, do you like your dress still?"

"Of course," she said with a wide-eyed smile, gesturing to the sleek black maid-of-honor dress she wore that McKenna had picked for her.

"It's totally you. I wanted you to have a dress you could wear again. Maybe to a date? A fancy night out?"

The words fell on her ears with a hollow clang. Because she could no longer wish for a night out with the man she wanted terribly.

Clay had left her that morning on the streets of San Francisco, ending their brief love affair and driving away in his town car. She couldn't fault him for taking off. She couldn't give him what he wanted—an end to her secrecy. That's what Clay needed more than anything. More than her body, more than their chemistry, more even than their endless nights together. She couldn't tell him the truth about why she'd lied to the guy with the gun who'd been waiting on her doorstep that morning when they had returned after breakfast. What could she say? *He's the mob heavy who's been assigned to me to make sure I pay off a debt that isn't even mine?* If she told Clay, he'd be a target too, because that's how these men operated: they circled you, ensnaring you on all sides until the people you loved fell into their crosshairs, too.

That's why she'd claimed Clay was just some guy she'd met in a bar, rather than a high-profile entertainment lawyer with an even higher-profile list of clients. She wanted to protect his identity and keep him out of the line of fire.

"And I will wear it again. Again and again. I promise," she said, tugging McKenna in for a warm embrace, even though she had no idea when or where she'd wear this number.

After they stepped out of their dresses, McKenna paid the final deposit on both, plunking down her credit card on the counter without a second thought. Julia felt a sliver of envy for the ease with which her sister could navigate matters of money. Shrewd businesswoman that she was, McKenna had turned her fashion blog into a fashion empire. If she'd owed a big, fat debt, it could be paid off instantly from her flush savings account. If she asked, McKenna would pay Julia's debt too, handing over the dough in a heartbeat. But she wasn't going to attach her sister to this problem because that's how it became hers in the first place—when it was passed on to her, like a disease.

"Chris said the meeting with Clay went great today," McKenna remarked as they strolled out of the shop and onto the busy street, crowded with mid-afternoon foot traffic: moms pushing strollers into coffee shops and young hipsters heading back to work after lunch at cafes with all-organic menus.

"That's great about the meeting," Julia said, as casually as she could.

"Did he tell you about it?"

"Chris? Why would I be talking to him?"

McKenna shoved her playfully. "Um, no. The hot guy you went to New York for. The hot guy I know you're into. Are you going to see Clay while he's in town?"

She shrugged and looked away, and those twin gestures were enough for her sister to stop in her tracks and park her hands on her hips. "Whoa. What's going on?"

And with that, it was as if a tight knot started to unravel in her. She might not be able to tell her sister about her money troubles, but she could at least let her know about her man woes.

"I did see him last night. I don't think it's going to work out between us," she said, and she didn't bother to strip the frustration from her voice, or the residual sadness. A sob threatened to lodge in her throat and turn into a fit of dumb waterworks. But giving in to the tears was like kicking a brick wall. It didn't do any good, and you were left mostly with a stubbed toe.

"Oh no. Why do you say that?"

"He's too far away in New York. And I'm just busy here. And he's all about work."

"That stinks," McKenna said, and she stomped her foot on the sidewalk. The gesture was so child-like that Julia couldn't help but laugh. "But at least you weren't too far in?" she said, her eyes full of hopefulness. She wrapped an arm around her sister.

Julia was tempted to reassure her. To tell her it was nothing, just a night here, a weekend there. But it wasn't. He was more, so much more.

"Actually, I really liked him a lot, so it's a bit of a bummer."

"Then we need to go drown our sorrows in French fries and cake. Let me take you out," McKenna offered.

Julia said yes, and though the French fries were fantastic, they weren't enough, not even close, to forget about the man she couldn't have. The problem was she didn't have any room in her life for him, and if she let him linger any more in her heart, she'd surely lose the game tonight.

Tonight was for winning.

CHAPTER TWO

The venture capitalist with the laughing tell was back, and he spent most of the game staring at Julia. But Hunter must have gotten a tip to strike that laugh from his repertoire because the first time he chuckled Julia went all in, and lost a cool grand. He'd really had three kings. No bluffing.

He'd likely snagged himself a poker tutor, some former pro player who now trained eager wannabe card sharks in the ways of the game, or a grizzled old veteran needing to earn a dime or two after he'd retired. She'd seen it before among the hotshots. A pivot here, a change-up there—all signs that they were being coached on the side. And that they thought they were hot shit.

He wasn't. No one was.

"I'm in," he said, shoving a black chip into the pot, eyes on her the whole time. Like she was his prey.

So wrong.

She was the predator. They were all her enemies, every last one of them, and just because she'd lost a hand didn't mean she was going to lose the game. She rubbed her index finger against a black chip, checked out her cards again, then scanned Hunter's face. Pale skin, pock marks from acne probably garnered only a few years ago when he was in high school, and a nice, straight nose. His blue eyes were locked on her, and that was another clue he'd hired a tutor. He'd probably been told to stare her down, the tutor thinking that would knock her off her game.

Didn't work. Not in general, and certainly not tonight, when she had jetpacks of anger fueling her. She was pissed at Dillon, pissed at Stevie, pissed at Charlie, pissed at Hunter, and most of all, pissed at Clay for not believing her. If only he could see her now, he'd feel like a goddamn heel for casting all that doubt on her. He'd acted like she was a lying drug user, like his ex. Ha. Couldn't be farther from the truth. She wished she could record this game with a secret hidden camera and show him. *"There. See? I'm this scumbag's ringer 'til my debt is done. Happy now?"*

Screw him and his lack of faith. Screw Hunter and his lack of a tell. Screw his tutor. Screw them all. She was ballsier than Hunter, and she'd play to her strengths. *Guts.*

She had two tens, and she was betting on them.

"I'll see your $500 and I'll raise you $1000," she said, pressing her long red fingernail against one chip, sliding it in, then methodically doing the same with the next two chips.

He showed no response for a few seconds, as if he were trying to hold in his reaction. Then his eyebrow twitched, and she wanted to pump a fist. New tell, perhaps?

The rest of the crew had folded. The guy who owned a sporting goods shop leaned back in his chair, eyes flickering between Julia and Hunter. He was a regular, and a plant. He won some, lost some, and generally was in attendance to balance out a game. There was also a young guy with chiseled cheekbones and wavy hair who drove one of Charlie's limos. All here to pad the table.

Over in the kitchen, Stevie the Skunk sifted through a plate of fresh-baked cookies, scarfing down another one. She had no idea who'd baked cookies for a rigged card game, but maybe it was his mama or his wife. Or maybe it was his colleague. There was a new guy with him, a baby-faced fellow named Max with gray eyes and a barrel-like body. *Perhaps he was a trainee of Skunk's*, Julia had mused when she'd met him before the game. No gun on his ankle yet, though. Maybe he hid it elsewhere.

Hunter surprised her by grabbing two chips and dropping them in the pile. "Time to show the cards. Lucky sevens," he said with a lopsided grin, all confidence and bravado now. She wondered if his tutor would pat him on the back for that move, and say *good boy.* She wondered if she cared what his tutor thought. She decided she didn't. All she wanted was that money, so badly she was damn near salivating for it. All those black beauties in the pile would bring her a touch closer to freedom from Charlie's thumb, and his knife, and his goon who followed her around with a gun.

She laid down her hand, revealing her pair of tens. Hunter nodded once, all steely-eyed and cool at first. But when Julia pulled the chips over to her corner of the table, he pointed a finger at her. She raised her eyes, mildly curious.

Hunter didn't speak at first. She could see the cogs in his head turning, like he was adding, multiplying and dividing.

"You don't play like the rest of them," he said in an even voice.

"You don't say," she replied, emotionless.

"You play like a shark. I see it in your eyes. I know that look. I'm a venture capitalist. I have that look every day when I take a risk. You're the same."

"Just call me a VC then," she said as she stacked her chips, keeping her hands steady even though her heart was thumping.

"You're not just a player," he said, with narrowed eyes.

"Call me a player. Call me not a player. I don't care. Why don't you just deal the next hand?" she said, keeping her cool as best she could.

Skunk looked up from the cookies when he heard the chatter. This was more talking than usual for this kind of a game.

"No," he said, shaking his head as he rose. "I'm not gonna deal. You're a fucking ringer, aren't you?"

Stevie the Skunk took the reins. He ambled over to the table and pressed his big hands on the wood. "What's going on? We all playing nice?"

"No. She's a ringer and this game is rigged. I knew something was up the first time, and I know it for sure now," he said, pointing his finger accusingly at the big man. Max marched closer but kept his distance, watching the scene.

Julia's blood raced along the speedways in her body, panic galloping through her veins. She had a sinking feeling about what was coming next, and she was right. Skunk reached for his gun with a speed she'd never imagined the lumbering man possessed. "Get the fuck out," he said coolly to Hunter. "And you're not welcome at the restaurant, either."

"I was right," Hunter said, practically hopping in righteousness.

Julia clamped her lips shut so she wouldn't shout, "*What did you think it was? What the hell else could this game possibly be?*"

"Charlie told me it was an executive game, but it's not," he insisted and he must have been the ballsiest VC in the Valley because he wasn't leaving.

Stevie waved the gun. "Was there something un-clear about what I said? Because it sounded clear to me. But if you're having trouble hearing, I'm happy to head on down to the local precinct tonight and make sure my friends on the force know that you put your fucking hands all over this woman here," he said, grip-ping Julia's shoulder with his free paw, in a gesture that felt both strangely protective and thoroughly in-vasive. "And I've got witnesses who'll vouch for me, right?"

The chiseled-cheekbone guy nodded along with the sporting goods fella.

The tiny hairs on the back of her neck stood on end, and she was oddly grateful for Skunk, and dis-gusted at the same time. He'd protected her, but he'd really protected Charlie's investment. And he'd done it in the same way Charlie had subverted her for his uses—by betting on her being a woman. By betting on men underestimating her at cards, and now by sug-gesting she was a helpless little lady who'd been man-handled.

Hunter grabbed his few remaining chips. "I'm cash-ing out."

"No you're not. You're getting out. That's your penalty for disrupting the game. Out," Skunk said in a low and powerful tone, pointing to the door.

Hunter held up his hands, huffed out through his nostrils. "You won't be seeing the last of me."

He left, the sound of his footsteps echoing as he clomped down the stairs.

* * *

Charlie glared at her. "What did you say to him?"

"I didn't say a thing."

"What did you say that made him figure it out?" Charlie pressed, dropping his chopsticks next to his plate of pork dumplings at the Chinese restaurant underneath the apartment where the game was held. The restaurant was empty. It had closed an hour ago.

"I told you. *Nothing.*"

"I don't need all of the VCs knowing our game is rigged. He and his friends come to my restaurant every Friday for lunch. Their employees eat here too," he said, stabbing the table with a finger. "I had some of his friends from Steiner Hawkins coming to the next game. They just sold a social media startup they backed for $50 million. They are flush with cash. You know what that means?"

Julia shook her head, fear rippling across her chest. "No."

Charlie pushed back from the table and rose. He stalked closer to Julia, forcing her to back up against the wall. He crowded her, caging her in with his hands on each side of her head.

"Let me explain what it means, Red," he said, spitting the words on her face. "It means they're not coming. They're not playing my game. It means I won't get their money. And that also means the next time you play, you take a fall."

"What?" She furrowed her brow in disbelief. "How does that help any of us?"

"It sends the word to the street that my games are fair. You take a fall. And you are in my debt, Red."

"I won tonight," she said, trying to insist. "I won $6,000. I'm close. I'm almost there."

"You didn't win $6,000," he said breathing on her. The scent of fried pork coming from his mouth curled her stomach. "You cost me $6,000."

She wanted to sink to the ground, to crouch down and hug her knees and curl up in a corner. She felt like she'd been smashed with an anvil. Every time she got closer, he moved the finish line.

"It's not even my debt," she said, her voice bordering on begging.

"It is your debt. I have seen your pretty little bar, with your pretty little bartenders, and my pretty little money that you put into it. And let me remind you of what happens if you ever think I will forget that you owe me."

He grabbed her by the hair and yanked. She stifled a scream, and her mind flashed to how different it felt when Clay pulled her hair or boxed her in against the wall. When he did those things it was fair and it was wanted, and it was part of the way they played with each other. There was no game with Charlie. He played to hurt, and he gripped her hair so tight she believed he had the strength to tug it right off her scalp.

He jerked her through the empty restaurant, out the door and into the foggy night, then down the block, stopping in front of a pub. He let go of her hair, and she wanted to cry with relief. "This bar? See this bar? Picture it as yours. It's Cubic Z, and if we're not clear by the end of the next month, it's mine."

"No!" she said, trembling from head to toe. She had employees; she had a co-owner. She was responsible for them all, for their livelihood, even for the little baby growing in Kim's belly.

"Yes," he said with an evil smile as he nodded vigorously. "Yes, it will be mine, and I have not decided if it will be Charlie Z or if I will simply take great pleasure in running it into the ground and then having my way with you." He stopped talking to coil a strand of her hair around his index finger. "I might be starting some new businesses with some very pretty women who can make money for me the old-fashioned way. Would you like that, Red? To be on your back?"

Every cell in her body screamed as fear plunged its way through her veins. "No," she said, her voice shaking.

"I didn't think so. Now get out of my sight."

He turned her around and shoved her hard on her spine. In her skyscraper heels, she stumbled and the sidewalk loomed ominously close, but she gripped the doorway of the bar in time, and walked away from him. When she reached her building, she stopped at the mailboxes in the lobby and grabbed bills, flyers and coupons. She quickly sorted the letters, tossing credit-card offers and carpet-cleaning deals in the trash. Then she spotted a letter that would make any citizen groan.

From the IRS.

She slid her finger under the flap as she trudged up the stairs, wondering what the government could want from her. She paid her taxes on time every year. She unfolded the letter and scanned it—a letter of inquiry. The IRS was asking if she knew where Dillon Whittaker was living these days since he hadn't filed his taxes for the year before.

She scoffed as she unlocked her door. If Charlie didn't know where Dillon was, the IRS sure as hell wasn't going to find him.

* * *

Later that night, the hot water from the shower rained down on her head and her mind returned to Dillon. When they'd met he seemed like the easygoing photographer, the funny guy with a quick wit, and a sweet word.

But he was so much more. He was insidious in ways she never imagined he could be, because he'd figured out how to leave town with $100,000 scot-free, and no strings attached. Tra la *fucking* la. She could still recall the moment when her world came crashing down. She and Dillon had already split, and she wasn't keeping tabs on him so she didn't know he'd fled the country. She'd been mixing a pitcher of margaritas for a bachelorette party when Charlie strolled into the bar, parking himself on a sleek, steel stool. He steepled his hands in front of him, and cocked his head to the side. "How is the expansion going?"

"What do you mean?" she asked curiously. She knew Charlie, had met him once before through Dillon, but they'd never broken bread or toasted together.

"I understand you needed some money for your bar. Dillon asked me for a loan on your behalf, and since he's been good and loyal to me, and was willing to pay 15 percent, I happily said yes. And seeing as Dillon has left the country, it seemed the right time for you and I to get acquainted."

The saying *you could hear a pin drop* took on new meaning as the sound in the bar was vacuumed up. She could hear everything, from the chatter of nearby patrons, to the waiters placing drinks on low tables, to the frantic beat of her heart and the blood roaring in her ears.

"What do you mean?" She carefully set down the pitcher she was holding. If she held it a second longer she'd drop it, and it would shatter and break. It would be her tell, and if there's one thing she knew from the mobster movies she'd seen, you don't let them smell your fear. When they do, they pounce.

He drummed his fingers against the counter. "What I mean is we need to talk, Red."

"About what?" she asked, feeling like an animal crouching in a corner.

"About what you can do to repay me."

Her eyes widened. "But the money wasn't for me. I didn't even know he got a loan from you," Julia had said, her voice rising in fear, her skin turning pale.

Charlie arched an eyebrow. "That's very funny."

"But it's true. This is the first I've heard of this, I swear. I never got that money. I never saw a dime. I had no idea," she said, trying so hard to prove her innocence, as her stomach twisted and her hands turned clammy.

This couldn't be happening.

Charlie cackled. "That's what they all say. *I had no idea.* But now it's time to have *an* idea about how you're going to pay me. I hear you like poker. Make me a gin and tonic and I will tell you how you will be playing for me. Because what this means, Red, is that you are mine."

She still was his, and she had no idea how much longer she would have to pay for that son-of-a-bitch's twisted act of deception.

* * *

Julia couldn't sleep, which bugged the crap out of her. She'd never suffered from insomnia, not even in the darkest days with Dillon. Not even in those early weeks of Charlie's indentured servitude when she was still dazed and shocked that this had become her life. But now she lay wide awake in her king-size bed, the window open, the late night sounds of San Francisco drifting in: the occasional car horn, the faint hum of the bus that ran on electricity, the crash of a garbage can, likely knocked over by a vagrant.

Clay had seemed a bit wary of her neighborhood, and while her section of The Mission wasn't bad per se, it hadn't yet come into its own. She didn't mind the seedier elements; she knew real danger didn't lie with the guy panhandling on the street corner. But she liked that Clay had a protective side, and a helpful side, too. He'd tried so hard to get her to open up the other day and tell him all her troubles. She'd been tempted. She could see herself laying them at his feet and serving them up for him to solve.

But then her problems would become his problems, and she couldn't abide by that. Dillon had sloughed off his garbage onto her, and she wasn't going to hot potato it on to someone else, especially someone she cared so deeply for. Because she did care for him. So much more than she'd planned to when she said yes to that one weekend in New York. She'd thought she could jet across the country and have a fantastic get-away. Instead, she'd gone all in.

She had nothing to show for it though.

All the anger that fueled her during the game had faded, and she simply felt weary, and lonely, too, as she flashed back to the pained look on his face, to the tortured gaze in his eyes, to the way he'd reacted when she'd pleaded.

Then she cast her mind further back to the night before when he'd tried so hard to find his way into her heart. Her chest tightened at the memory, and she longed so deeply to let him in the way he wanted, and the way she wanted too.

The very least she could do was say she was sorry. She grabbed her phone from her nightstand and began tapping out a message to the man she missed more than she had ever expected.

CHAPTER THREE

As he stepped off the red-eye from Los Angeles to New York the next morning, his email burst with a flurry of messages.

First, a note from Flynn about the Pinkertons, and how the deal was coming together for their next film. Then one from his friend Michele, reminding him that they had tickets to the theater in a week. Damn, he'd nearly forgotten they were going to see an adaptation of *The Usual Suspects* for the stage. Next, a quick update from an actor client, Liam, who was starring in that play and also opening a hip restaurant in Murray Hill. Clay had been advising him on the deal. Liam was a busy guy and Clay liked it that way. Then a note from Chris McCormick, the TV show host he'd met with in San Francisco after spending one more night with Julia.

One unforgettable night that had as much to do with her answering the door wearing only stockings and a shirt as it did with her finally starting to open up to him.

But that had all been a lie, he reminded himself, willing his heart to fossilize when it came to her. Telling himself not to linger on the memories of how she seemed to be sharing her fears, and inviting him into her life, because that was all upended when she lied about who he was to that thug on the street.

His fingers tightened on his phone, gripping it harder, as if he were channeling his frustration into the screen. He needed to get into Manhattan as soon as possible, make a pit stop at his boxing gym, and then get his ass to work. That was his plan of attack: the way to rid Julia from his mind. Head down, nose in work, client meetings—the recipe to numb him to the effect of that woman.

He scrolled through Chris's note, a quick summary of what he was most looking for in his next contract with the TV network that carried his show, and then he read Chris's previous contract that the host had handled on his own. *As you can probably surmise, negotiating on my own behalf is not my expertise. Happy to have you doing it for me going forward*, Chris had written.

He replied quickly to Chris, eager to prove his value to his new client. That the guy was marrying Julia's sister in a month didn't even factor into his decision. Because he wasn't thinking about Julia, not as he walked past security, responding to a note, not as he found his driver while answering another email, and certainly not as he slid into the backseat of a town car that would zip him into the city.

Then he saw a new email land in his inbox. From her. The subject line gave nothing away: *Hi.* But Pavlovian response kicked in, and he opened it before he could think. Because seeing her name still felt like a damn good thing, still held the promise of a sexy note, a naughty line, or a sweet nothing. But more than any of those options, it held the promise of *her.*

from: purplesnowglobe@gmail.com
to: cnichols@gmail.com
date: April 25, 4:08 AM
subject: Hi

Clay,

Hi. I'm lying awake in bed thinking of last night. How only 24 hours ago you were here with me. How much better it was to sleep with your arms around me, all safe and warm and snug. How much I would love to have you here again. But I know that won't happen. And I understand. I truly understand. If I were you, I would hate me too. If I were you, I'd be suspicious as hell. And I probably wouldn't trust me either. So I get 100 percent where you're coming from and I wish there were another way. I want you in my life so badly that I can feel this ache where you're supposed to be. But I know I can't have you, and I'm sorry I can't be open right now. You deserve more than this. More than me. All I will say is this sucks, and if I could turn back time and do certain things over there's a lot I would change.

But I wouldn't change a second with you.

Wow. I just re-read my note. I think that's the mushiest I've ever been with anyone. Damn, you did a number on me, and I've got it bad for you. I'm hitting send while I still have the guts in me to do so, even though I will probably regret it. Except this is all true.

Xoxo
Julia

He dropped his head in his hand, and cursed. A wave of frustration and longing rolled through him, and he knew he should turn the damn phone off and ignore her. But this woman, she was under his skin. He hated lies but he'd be lying to himself if he pretended he'd forgotten her in a day.

from: cnichols@gmail.com
to: purplesnowglobe@gmail.com
date: April 25, 7:12 AM
subject: Hi

I don't hate you. The farthest thing from it.

He hit send before the regret washed over him, as it eventually would, he was sure.

* * *

By the end of the day he wasn't feeling much. He was riding at the perfect levels of blankness. A day in the trenches had done wonders for him, and a night at the gym would drain him of any residual feelings that threatened to resurface.

The next day he did the same, burying himself in business, making sure every *T* was crossed and *I* dotted, that points were won, and clients weren't just making more money, they were being protected in their business deals. His job was a hell of a lot more than wringing more dollars from networks, studios and producers. It was checking out the fine print, making sure clients were looked out for when it came to two, three, four years down the road in a deal.

His days followed that pattern for the next week, and the regular routine of work, gym, business drinks or dinner, sleep, then rinse, lather, repeat the next day turned Julia into a hazy blur in the rearview mirror. Soon, she'd migrated to the back of his mind, and the fact that she'd been relocated there pleased him immensely. A few more days of supreme focus and she would be a distant blip on the horizon.

At seven-thirty on the dot on a Wednesday night, he left his office and headed for Times Square, threading his way through the crowds of tourists in their *I*

Love NY sweat-shirts and *Property of NYFD* nylon jackets, with pretzels and hot dogs in hand, as they snapped photos of the neon signs and the famous intersection. He walked past the St. James Theater, tapping once on the poster for *Crash the Moon*, feeling a surge of pride for that show's quick success. His friend Davis had directed it, and it had become a smash hit in the first month alone, playing to packed houses every single night.

He crossed the street, dodging a cab stalled in traffic, as he made his way to the bright lights of the Shubert Theater where Liam was playing the Kevin Spacey character in *The Usual Suspects*. Michele waited outside the theater lobby, smiling when she spotted him, and Clay took some comfort in the reliability of a friend like her. She'd been here through the years, always available for a drink, always willing to chat, or to see a movie or show. She was a good one, steady, dependable, and patently honest. A warm feeling rushed over him with the reminder that there were people you could trust implicitly. She would never dance around the truth.

"Hey you," she said, waving her fingers, and then giving him a quick kiss on each cheek.

"Are we French now?"

"Of course," she said playfully. "We'll grab baguettes and sip espresso after the curtain call."

"That'd be nice," he said, as they walked into the theater and he handed two tickets to the usher who led them down the aisle to some of the best seats in the house.

Michele raised an eyebrow. "Impressive."

"Like this is a surprise? We always get the best seats. Your brother is a Tony-winning director," Clay said, gesturing for Michele to take her seat.

"I know. And I don't ever take that for granted. And you," she said, wrapping her hand around his arm, and leaning in close, "are the man behind the scenes who makes this stuff happen, too."

He waved off the compliment. He wasn't in the business for compliments. "Tell me about your day," he said, and listened as she shared the little details that she could, not breaking any client confidentiality but talking in general terms about her work listening to the woes of others as one of New York's finest shrinks. Her voice was calming and soothing, so he barely noticed that she'd kept her hand on his forearm the whole time.

When the curtain rose at the start of the play, she stayed like that, palm wrapped around him. A few minutes into the first act, he almost asked her to move her hand, but then it wasn't really bothering him, and they were old friends. Even if they'd kissed once back in college, it didn't matter that she was touching him, shifting closer. Her shoulder was brushing his by the time the cast took their bows. *She smelled nice*, he thought. Some flowery scent to her hair, maybe jasmine? He'd never noticed it before.

"Did you like the play?" he asked as the theater rang with cheers for the actors.

"Loved it."

"Never gets old, does it? Even when you know it's coming, the Keyser Soze reveal."

"It's a brilliant twist," she said, agreeing.

"I need to go see Liam." He gestured to the backstage entrance. "You gonna come along?"

"Of course."

Once backstage, Liam greeted him with a clap on the back and a hearty hug.

"Nice work. You were better than Spacey," Clay said.

Liam beamed and pointed his index finger at Clay. "Flattery will get you everywhere." Then he turned to Michele. "And who is the lovely lady on your arm tonight?"

Michele laughed nervously. "Oh, we're not together. Just friends," she said, extending a hand to shake.

Liam's green eyes twinkled. "All the better for me," he said, then ran a hand through his mass of dark hair. "Why don't you come along to The Vitale then for a nightcap? It's right next to the restaurant I'll be opening soon."

Clay wanted to roll his eyes. Could Liam be any more obvious? But Michele seemed to be enjoying it because she answered quickly. "I would love to."

"I would love to take you."

Liam was recognized a few times on the street, and again at the bar where he was amiable, and signed a cocktail napkin for a young woman who said she was a theater student at NYU and had always loved his work.

"That's so nice that she adores you so much," Michele said to Liam when the woman walked away.

"And I adore signing cocktail napkins," Liam said, with his trademark grin that made women swoon. "Signed a few in the Bahamas last weekend."

"How was your vacation there?" Clay asked. "Good times?"

"Amazing. Gorgeous blue skies, perfect weather . . . did some fishing. Oh, and listen to this. Some guy tried to get me to buy real estate there. A damn condo, of all things," Liam said, tossing his hands up in exasperation. "Do they think I was born yesterday? I know how those things work. It was probably for one of those deals where only one unit is done so they show you that. And then just pictures of the rest."

"And you want me to advise you on whether this is a good deal or not?" Clay said in a dry tone.

"Oh yeah. Exactly. Please tell me, because my poor little actor brain can't figure it out," he said, and the two men laughed.

"Actually," Michele chimed in, crossing her legs, and sitting up straighter in the bar stool as she kept her eyes locked on Liam. "I've heard that a lot of those scams try to prey on celebrities. Because so many celebrities can often make quick decisions with money."

"I can make quick decisions on other things," Liam said, waggling his eyebrows at Michele.

"Like what, Liam?" she asked in a soft, sexy voice Clay had rarely heard her use.

Damn, the flirting between the two was stirring up again. "And that's my cue to go," Clay said, slapping some money down on the bar. He patted Liam on the shoulder. "Poker tomorrow night?"

"Of course."

"See you then."

He started to leave, but Michele followed him to the doorway. "You're always just taking off," she said brusquely, crossing her arms.

"Didn't seem I was necessary around here. You two are hitting it off," he said with a shrug.

"Are you trying to pawn me off on him?"

"Pawn you off?" he asked as if she'd been speaking a foreign language. "You guys are getting along. I'm making myself scarce so you can keep getting along."

She heaved a sigh. "How was your trip to San Francisco last week?"

He could have done without the reminder. It took every ounce of will he had to strip his California girl from his brain. "It was fine."

"Did you ever hear from that woman you were crazy about?"

And his perfect hold on not thinking about Julia slipped through his fingers. One mention, one reminder of how he felt for her, and she came roaring back to the front of his mind. It was like a truck had slammed into his body, the weight and pressure of the memory of the woman he craved. "Michele, if you don't want to hang with Liam, I don't care. I'll tell him I need to take you home. Whatever you need. I'm not trying to pawn you off on him. I thought you were having a nice time with him and I wanted to get out of the way. If I read the signals wrong, I'm sorry."

"You do a lot of that, don't you?" she said, looking him fiercely in the eyes like they were locked in a battle to not blink first.

He squinted at her, as if that would help him understand what she was saying. "What do you mean?"

"Read the signals wrong, Clay. You read the signals wrong," she said, parking her hands on her hips.

"What signals am I reading wrong?"

"You really don't get it, do you?"

He shook his head in frustration. "Evidently I don't. And on that note, it was a pleasure spending the evening with you."

Once he returned to his home, he tossed his suit jacket on the couch, unbuttoned his shirt, and threw it in the laundry. He washed his face, brushed his teeth, shed the rest of his clothes, and then flopped down on his bed, surrounded by the sounds of silence.

He considered taking up meditation for a nanosecond. Then practicing a mantra. Hell, maybe he could even give yoga a shot. But in the end, none of those things suited him, so he did what his instincts told him to do. Reach out to Julia.

CHAPTER FOUR

from: cnichols@gmail.com
to: purplesnowglobe@gmail.com
date: May 2, 8:23 PM
subject: You

I keep thinking about what happened on your street. Can't stop worrying about you. Are you okay?

from: purplesnowglobe@gmail.com
to: cnichols@gmail.com
date: May 2, 11:24 PM
subject: Me

Mostly. How are you?

from: cnichols@gmail.com
to: purplesnowglobe@gmail.com
date: May 2, 8:25 PM
subject: Not my favorite day that's for sure

Been better . . .

from: purplesnowglobe@gmail.com
to: cnichols@gmail.com
date: May 2, 11:26 PM
subject: Wish I could change that

I hate the thought of you having a bad day. I want
you to be happy.

from: cnichols@gmail.com
to: purplesnowglobe@gmail.com
date: May 2, 8:27 PM
subject: I'm not unhappy

I'm just worried about you. I feel like an ass. Like I
just left you there on the street.

from: purplesnowglobe@gmail.com
to: cnichols@gmail.com
date: May 2, 11:29 PM
subject: You're not, but you have a nice ass :)

I'm a big girl. I made it home safely. But it's sweet
you were worried.

from: cnichols@gmail.com
to: purplesnowglobe@gmail.com
date: May 2, 8:31 PM
subject: Sweet? Me?

I still am worried. Is Stevie bugging you?

from: purplesnowglobe@gmail.com
to: cnichols@gmail.com
date: May 2, 11:32 PM
subject: Soooo sweet . . . strong, confident, sexy too

He's fine. It will all be fine soon enough. Let's talk about something else. I came up with a new cocktail tonight.

from: cnichols@gmail.com
to: purplesnowglobe@gmail.com
date: May 2, 8:33 PM
subject: Mixing it up

Tell me about it.

from: purplesnowglobe@gmail.com
to: cnichols@gmail.com
date: May 2, 11:34 PM
subject: Delish on your lips . . .

It's lemonade, vodka and champagne.

from: cnichols@gmail.com
to: purplesnowglobe@gmail.com
date: May 2, 8:35 PM
subject: That describes you . . .

Sounds like something I'd never touch but that will be beloved by your bar goers.

from: purplesnowglobe@gmail.com
to: cnichols@gmail.com
date: May 2, 11:36 PM
subject: Love your innuendo

It is already. The gal I run the bar with served a ton tonight. Said it was a big hit. Everyone was happy-buzzed too.

from: cnichols@gmail.com
to: purplesnowglobe@gmail.com
date: May 2, 8:37 PM
subject: Double entendres too

Sounds like a perfect state of existence. Can I have one of those too? The happy-buzz, that is.

from: purplesnowglobe@gmail.com
to: cnichols@gmail.com
date: May 2, 11:37 PM
subject: Named it for you

I call it The Heist. What did you do tonight? If you were on a date, please just tell me you played with kittens at a rescue shelter or something instead.

from: cnichols@gmail.com
to: purplesnowglobe@gmail.com
date: May 2, 8:39 PM
subject: No pussy tonight

I saw a play. My favorite kind of storyline. (And thank you for the name. Maybe I will taste it some-time)

from: purplesnowglobe@gmail.com
to: cnichols@gmail.com
date: May 2, 11:41 PM
subject: Keep it that way!

The kind with a plot twist?

from: cnichols@gmail.com
to: purplesnowglobe@gmail.com
date: May 2, 8:42 PM
subject: Good memory

Yes. Call me impressed.

from: purplesnowglobe@gmail.com
to: cnichols@gmail.com
date: May 2, 11:44 PM
subject: You are on my mind

I remember everything about you . . . So . . . is today
getting better for you?

from: cnichols@gmail.com
to: purplesnowglobe@gmail.com
date: May 2, 8:46 PM
subject: Yes. Since 20 minutes ago

Now it is.

from: purplesnowglobe@gmail.com
to: cnichols@gmail.com
date: May 2, 11:48 PM
subject: What was your favorite day ever?

Tell me a favorite memory from when you were
younger. Pumpkin patch visit as a boy in Vegas?
Lettering in varsity football? Prom? I bet you were
prom king.

from: cnichols@gmail.com
to: purplesnowglobe@gmail.com
date: May 2, 8:49 PM
subject: I was not . . .

But I looked good in a blue ruffly tux.

from: purplesnowglobe@gmail.com
to: cnichols@gmail.com
date: May 2, 11:50 PM
subject: Pictures please

Dying to see THAT.

from: cnichols@gmail.com
to: purplesnowglobe@gmail.com
date: May 2, 8:51 PM
subject: Lawyers don't send pictures

I know better than to send self-incriminating evidence.

from: purplesnowglobe@gmail.com
to: cnichols@gmail.com
date: May 2, 11:53 PM
subject: Damn that lawyer photo clause

I will just have to imagine you in your tux, and even though you were probably an insanely hot teenage boy, I suppose I really should be perving on you as a man. An insanely hot man. And you probably look insanely hot in a tux.

from: cnichols@gmail.com
to: purplesnowglobe@gmail.com
date: May 2, 8:55 PM
subject: Tux fetish?

I suspect any tux I wore would look best with your hands on the buttons.

from: purplesnowglobe@gmail.com
to: cnichols@gmail.com
date: May 2, 11:56 PM
subject: You fetish

Unbuttoning them.

from: cnichols@gmail.com
to: purplesnowglobe@gmail.com
date: May 2, 9:02 PM
subject: Dangerous ground

We shouldn't be doing this . . .

from: purplesnowglobe@gmail.com
to: cnichols@gmail.com
date: May 3, 12:04 AM
subject: Say the word

Do you want me to stop?

from: cnichols@gmail.com
to: purplesnowglobe@gmail.com
date: May 2, 9:05 PM
subject: Don't stop

No . . .

He told himself he was safe from her web of lies and brand of hurt by the three thousand miles that separated them. As long as he stayed a continent away, he'd be okay. So when her name flashed across the screen with the enticing words—incoming call—he answered immediately.

"Hello."

"Hi," she said in a sleep-sexy purr.

"Are you in bed?"

"Only place I like to be when I'm talking to you," she said, and he loved knowing what she looked like all stretched out on her bed. Like an invitation. A beautiful fucking invitation for him with those long, strong legs, her curvy hips, her beautiful breasts, and that gorgeous red hair spread out on the covers.

"I bet you're wearing something sexy. Some little lingerie or bra-and-panty set," he said, keeping the talk to sexiness because he couldn't handle anything more right now.

"Do you want to know?"

"I want you to paint the image in my eye."

"I have on my bare legs."

A bolt of heat shot through his body, as he pictured her. "I like it when you wear those."

"And I hope you're not disappointed, but I don't have on a bra."

An appreciative growl escaped his throat. "Mmm. That is an excellent look on you. You do bra-lessness well. And now I'm picturing those naked shoulders of yours, kissing you all over, nibbling on your collarbone."

"Biting down," she said, continuing their imaginary travels.

"You taste so good, Julia. So sweet. Your skin is so damn sweet all over," he said, and the memory of her taste rushed back to him, blasting into him like a collision of senses in his memory. Her collarbone, the fruity smell of her hair from whatever shampoo she used, so much more enticing than any other woman's, the smell of her legs when she'd stepped out of the bath. And most of all, the scent of her arousal. The way he could tell just from inhaling her how he'd turned her on.

"Don't you want to know what else I'm wearing?" she offered, her voice as naughty as could be.

He stretched out on his own bed, and parked his free hand behind his head. He was so hard right now from picturing her, but he had to restrain himself because he knew he couldn't have her. But maybe this kind of teasing would be enough to get her out of his system. He knew this was trouble, he'd been there before, but this woman allured him like no other. She was a sexy drug and he wanted another hit.

"I do want to know," he said, his voice a low rumble.

"Hold on a sec," she said, and he heard a scatter of movement on her end. Then her voice again. "Go see."

Those two words shot straight to his groin, and he was fighting a losing battle with resistance when he scrolled to his screen, and thumbed open his text message to find a picture. A flash of white lace, a glimpse of her hipbone, and then her hand just barely dipped into the waistband of her panties. Suggesting what she was about to do if things continued.

Did he want them to?

No. And yes. And no. And yes. But as he tried to retain the reasons for hanging up, they all fell to dust when she whispered, "I'm touching myself and I'm thinking of you."

He groaned, unbidden. Everything in him craved her. Needed her. "Tell me what you're thinking."

She didn't answer right away, only breathed once, a low, sexy moan. In the span of those seconds, images flashed before him—her tied up to his bed, her bent over his desk, handcuffed to his balcony. Him pleasuring her, owning her body.

"Kissing you," she whispered, and his blood stilled because he'd been expecting something dirtier from her sexy mouth.

"Yeah? You like that?"

"I wouldn't like any of the other things if I didn't like kissing you first," she said, a gasp escaping her.

"What do you like about the way I kiss you?"

"Everything. Every single thing. Your lips are soft, and your stubble is rough, and you know exactly how to kiss me and make me melt for you," she said, and something about her voice was different this time; needier, hungrier.

"I love it when you melt into my arms," he said. "When I first see you and first kiss you."

"And it's like lightning or electricity or something," she said, and her breathing intensified.

"Like we can't get enough of each other, and can't stop kissing," he said, and a shudder wracked his body. "Tell me where your hand is now."

"Between my legs. Moving faster," she said, and let out a sexy cry that sent heat waves throughout his bones and blood.

"Are you writhing there on your bed?"

"Yes."

"With your legs wide open?"

"Yes," she said, her voice rising higher, and he could tell she was getting closer. "Are you touching yourself, Clay?"

"No," he said, though he was sure he'd need to handcuff his wrists any second to keep from grabbing his erection.

"Please," she said, her voice a delicious beg. That beg unwound him. It reached deep into his dirty mind and made him want to do everything with her, for her, to her.

"Please what?"

"Please touch yourself," she moaned, and he pictured her rocking her hips into her hand. With that image burned in front of his eyes, her voice in his ear, he knew it wouldn't take long. A few quick strokes, and he'd be there.

"Why do you want me to?"

"I like picturing you touching yourself. I like the image of your big, strong hand wrapped around your cock. Stroking yourself. Thinking of me."

"Yeah? That gets you hot?" His hands were trembling. He wanted so badly to give in to this moment with her.

"So hot. Anything you do turns me on. Don't you get that?"

"I think you just want to break me down. And make me think of you."

"But you already are, aren't you?"

"I already am," he admitted.

"Then come with me."

"What makes you think I'm going to come?"

"Because I know you. You will when you hear me in about thirty seconds," she said, and words fell away. She'd been reduced to moans and cries and pants, and there was no fucking way he could resist. It was either a cold shower for the rest of the whole night, or taking matters into his own hands. So he did, and it didn't take long for him to join her, pleasure rippling through every single vein as she cried out his name and he came hard and fast.

A minute later, after he'd washed his hands and returned to the dark of the bedroom, she spoke. "I wish I were there wearing your clothes right now."

He laughed. "That's what you want to be doing? Because I'd like to be fucking you if you were here."

"Well, that too. But then I'd put on your shirt."

"You like that, don't you?"

"I know you do too," she said.

"I do. Seeing you in my shirt and your heels is my kryptonite."

"Oh, is that it? That's your kryptonite?"

"Or maybe it's just that you are," he whispered, admitting more than he wanted to.

"I think the same could be said here."

There was a pause, and though they were three thousand miles apart, the silence was heady. He was in a drugged-out state tonight. This woman was his pill, and closeness with her was what he craved most even as he feared she would destroy his heart. Smash it to a million tiny pieces and eat it for lunch. But he had a built-in barrier in distance, and with no trips to San Francisco on his immediate calendar he saw nothing wrong with this temporary moment of relief from the pressure inside of him from wanting her. They couldn't be together in any meaningful way, and he couldn't get hurt if he didn't actually see her. Right? *Right*, he answered for himself.

"What are we doing, Julia?" he asked, and he was sure she could hear the longing in his tone, but he didn't care. There was no need to hide it after they'd just broken down and pleasured themselves together.

"I wish I knew," she said, her voice wistful and full of yearning. "I really wish I knew."

He heaved a sigh, trying to sort out his thoughts, but his brain was a mixed-up mess and he didn't know how to untangle all the threads. Or if he wanted to remain tangled up with her instead.

"What are you going to do when we hang up?" he asked, changing direction.

"Read a book."

"What are you reading these days?"

"A crazy story about a guy who treks across Antarctica."

"That does sound crazy."

"Yeah. He's kind of hallucinating and talking to penguins right now," she said with a small laugh.

"Can you blame him? I have to imagine if you're stuck in the polar ice cap that talking to penguins might be a rare source of comfort."

"As long as he doesn't eat the penguins I'll keep reading it."

"Here's to no penguin meals in the books we read."

"What will you do?"

"I suspect I will fall fast asleep and dream of a beautiful redhead on the other side of the country."

"She would like that dream very much," she said in a sweet voice, the kind that worked its way beneath all the hard edges in him, and settled deep in his heart. "Will I talk to you again soon?"

He took a fueling breath, and put his armor back on, steeling himself. "I don't know the answer to that."

CHAPTER FIVE

The next month passed in a paradoxical fashion. The days were long, but the weeks sped by as Julia won and lost for Charlie. She took the fall he asked for, but mostly she won, clearing another few thousand off her debt. The rest of the time, Julia mixed drinks at Cubic Z where she listened to Kim discuss whether to decorate the baby's nursery with horse or teddy bear wallpaper.

"Craig wants teddy bears. He says horses are too scary for little kids," Kim said, referring to her husband who helped out around the bar now and then as he looked for a regular bartending gig.

"Can I vote for otters instead?" Julia offered. "Have you ever seen an otter that's not utterly adorable?"

Kim laughed. "Can't say I've ever technically *seen* an otter at all. But I will hunt out otter wall-art now."

Julia held up her arms in the victory sign. "Ladies and gentleman, my greatest accomplishment may indeed lie in convincing my friend Kim to go for the otters."

She also helped her sister with final wedding prep, which included last-minute visits to boutiques and stores as McKenna chose gifts for the guests. No gifts for herself, though; McKenna and Chris had specifically asked for none, with the invitation saying, *Your presence is our gift. In lieu of presents, please consider a donation to your local animal shelter.*

Tonight, she popped into the bar to bring Julia a sample of cake. "I changed my mind at the last minute. I think I want to get this cake. Try it," she said, thrusting the carton across the bar.

Julia reached for a fork and took a bite, and her eyes rolled in pleasure when the sweet cake hit her tongue. "This is amazing."

McKenna clapped. "Oh good! Wedding cake is usually awful. But I want to have an amazing cake."

"Speaking of amazing things, try my newest concoction." She whipped up a Heist and slid it across the bar. "I named it for Clay," she said in an offhand way.

McKenna's eyebrows rose. "Wait! Are you back together with him?"

She shook her head. "No. We talk on the phone sometimes though," she said, adding an olive to the martini she'd just made for another customer.

"What do you talk about?" McKenna asked, her voice dripping with curiosity.

Julia shrugged playfully, remembering the late-night conversations with him, the way his voice went low and husky when he asked her what she was wearing, then when he proceeded to tell her exactly what he wanted to do to her when he'd removed every last shred of her clothing. "This and that." She handed the drink to the customer and returned to her sister.

"Are you having phone sex with him?" McKenna whispered, her eyes wide and eager for a yes.

She nodded. "And we talk too. About whatever. Our days. Movies. Books. Life. That sort of thing."

"Wow," McKenna said and her jaw was hanging open. "So are you going to see him again?"

"I think he likes the barrier. I think he probably figures it's for the best."

"Why?" McKenna asked, holding up a hand as if to say *what gives*. "I don't get it. You like him. He likes you. You have great phone sex. What is stopping the two of you from getting together?"

Instinctively, Julia's eyes flashed to the door, checking for Charlie or Skunk. Neither was there, but they might show up any day. That was the real thing keeping her and Clay apart. Keeping her distant from everyone, come to think of it.

"Who knows," she said evasively as a gray-haired and sharp-dressed man in a suit and tie raised a finger to grab her attention. "I need to go tend to some other customers. Can't wait for more cake this weekend."

She headed to the other end of the bar, slapped down a napkin, and flashed a smile at the older gentleman. "What can I get for you tonight?"

"A friend of mine tells me you make the most amazing cocktail ever," the man said, speaking in a most proper voice. He didn't have an accent per se; he simply had an air of sophistication about him, from the well-tailored suit to the classy speech. "A Purple Snow Globe, I believe?"

"Indeed. One Purple Snow Globe coming right up."

She mixed the drink and deposited it in front of him. When she returned five minutes later to check in, his eyes were sparkling and he was licking his lips. "That is a divine creation," he told her, then extended a hand. "I'm Glen Mills. I'm sure you'll be hearing from me soon."

"Why will I be hearing from you soon, Glen? You gonna offer me a job at some swank new bar you're opening?" she asked playfully.

"Not exactly," he said, with a twinkle in his eye, then he pushed off from the stool, and walked away.

She shook her head in amusement. The things men said in bars never surprised her, nor did she ever put any faith in them. Something about his name felt familiar though. *Glen Mills.* The named nagged at her brain for a spell, and she turned it over several times, like a strange object she could decipher if she looked at it from another angle, but she couldn't recall where she'd heard it before, so she let it go.

* * *

She could picture him perfectly when he told her he was crashed out on his couch, his shoulders sore in the way he liked from a hard workout tonight. She imagined him freshly showered, in shorts and a T-shirt, a combo she rarely saw her sharp-dressed man in, but a fantastic look nonetheless.

"Tell me why you like boxing," Julie said, as she closed the door to the tiny office at Cubic Z, slipping away for a short break while Kim handled the bar during a quiet time. She was spending her rare free minutes her favorite way. Talking to Clay. It wasn't the same as being in the room with him, but he was a far better phone date than any in-person date she'd ever had with another man. Though, he didn't call these stolen chats *dates*. He didn't call them anything. Maybe because the two of them were so undefined right now. They took what they could get from each other, but didn't push too far.

"Because I have to use my mind and my body," he said.

"Mmm. Two of the things I like about you." She sank down into the office chair, leaning back against it, letting his voice warm her. "And how do you use your mind when you're hitting a bag?"

"You have to focus with boxing. You have to know exactly where to land a punch, and then deliver on it."

"How did you get into boxing in the first place?"

"In high school."

"I thought you played football in high school?"

"I did. But I had no choice about boxing. Brent did it."

"And that meant you had to?"

"Can't let my little brother beat me. I had to keep up with him. Wouldn't let him have the chance to win. So I took it up too."

"I can beat McKenna if I have to," Julia joked.

"Girl fight. Don't get me excited," he said playfully.

"But I like getting you excited."

"And you're very good at it. You excel at that," he said, then paused and she heard the slightest rustling sound.

"You stretching out on the couch?"

"I'm making myself more comfortable."

"Do your shoulders still hurt?"

"A little."

She sighed wistfully, her eyes fluttering closed as she imagined being there with him, soothing out the soreness from the punches he'd thrown. "If I were there I'd rub your shoulders for you. You could lean back into me and I'd make you feel better."

"Mmm...I bet you would."

"You can rest your head between my legs while I massage you."

He laughed. "If I'm between your legs, there's no massaging going on. Unless it's of you and with my tongue."

She smiled and rolled her eyes. "Always able to make things dirty, aren't you, Clay?"

"If you're going to start talking about being between your legs, I'm going to start telling you what I'd be doing if I were there, and it wouldn't be lying still."

"What would it be?" She asked, unable to resist drawing out his naughty mouth.

"Wait. I *would* be lying still, now that I think about it," he said, quickly correcting himself.

"Oh really?"

"Yes, really. Because I'm tired, but I'm never to tired to eat you. I'd just need you to ride my face," he said. Hot tingles roared down her body at the memory of the ways he'd buried his face between her legs. On the chaise lounge in her bar after closing time the night they met, in the town car when she'd arrived in New York for their weekend together, and tied up on his bed, her ass in the air. Heat flooded her center, and she was going to need to change her panties before she went back out to work if this kept up.

"But maybe I want to do things to you," she said, taking the reins, so she didn't turn into a puddle of molten heat.

"All right. Have at me. What do you want to do to me?"

Her ears tuned into the noises from beyond the door. It sounded like more customers had just come in. She'd need to get back out there soon.

"Besides rub your shoulders and run my fingers through your hair?"

"Yes. Besides that."

"My favorite thing," she said in a sexy whisper, closing her eyes and picturing exactly what she wanted to do to him.

"What's your favorite thing, Julia? Tell me. I want to hear you say it."

"Tasting you."

He groaned, and she was sure his hand was already on his cock.

"Taking you in my mouth. Doing all sorts of things to you with my lips and tongue."

"What sort of things?"

"Taking you deep the way you like. Licking you all over. Using my hands everywhere on you."

"Everywhere?" he asked, and she could practically see him arching an eyebrow.

"Everywhere you'd want me to," she said, and soon his breathing intensified. "Are you touching yourself?"

"You leave me no choice when you talk about sucking me. I love those sexy lips of yours wrapped around my dick."

"And you love using your hands on me too while you're in my mouth. Grabbing my hair, pushing your fingers through it, pulling me closer to you."

"Making sure you take me hard," he growled.

"Of course. I want to make sure I rock your world with my mouth."

He drew a sharp breath, and she could tell he was getting close. "You do, Julia. You do."

"I can almost taste you right now," she said in a hot whisper, wanting to bring him there.

"You should be able to any second now," he said, breathing out hard, and groaning loudly.

She grinned widely, thrilled that she'd gotten him off like this. "You taste so fucking good," she said.

He sighed deeply, the sound of a contented man. She loved that she'd found a way to satisfy him even from this kind of distance. "Your turn," he said in that deep, sexy voice that sent sparks through her.

She shook her head even though he couldn't see her. "I need to get back to work. It's getting busy."

"Next time then. Because I want to hear you let go," he said, and a hot wave rolled through her as she pictured their nights on the phone, and how he drew out her cries of pleasure. "I love how you let go when you touch yourself."

"Why would I do anything else?"

"I want you to let go with me."

"I do, Clay. I've never held back."

"I don't mean sex. I mean other ways. I want you to be as free with me in other ways as you are when you're naked."

"I want that too. I swear I do," she said, and she was sure her neediness was coming through loud and clear. But she *needed* him to know. "I miss you."

"Yeah?" he asked, sounding doubtful.

"So much. I wish you were here with me."

He sighed heavily. "I wish I could be," he said, but it didn't sound as if he were wishing he could be there right now so he could touch her. More like he was wishing he would allow himself to be close to her again. Because in spite of all their late-night chats, and all the things they shared, there was a distance between them more palpable than the miles. She'd been getting to know him better, and yet, she had never felt farther away from him than she did now. "I have to go," he said, and now it *was* possible to feel even more distant.

When their call ended, she knew it couldn't go on much longer like this; this in-between state was wonderful and thoroughly unsatisfying at the same time.

CHAPTER SIX

Before the wedding she played another poker game. She was on some kind of streak the last few weeks, and she won most nights. "I only have $10,000 left," she said to Charlie at the end of the cash out. She couldn't hide the smile that curved her lips.

"You can count. But I also gave you a deadline and you have two more weeks to clear it."

"May isn't over yet," she said through gritted teeth.

"You could always ask your sister. I did a little research on her business. Seems she sold it for a pretty penny. Or perhaps you could just transfer your debt to the peppy Fashion Hound," he said, narrowing his eyes as he crisply punctuated the name of McKenna's fashion blog, making it clear he knew everything about the people she cared about. "I could find all sorts of ways for her to work for me. She has a nice dog, too."

Julia snapped, lunging for Charlie's throat in the restaurant. "Leave my sister and her dog out of this."

He cackled, grabbing her hands and flicking them off his skin. "I won't have to involve anyone if you do your job, Red."

She was tempted to ask McKenna for a loan, but she'd gotten this far on her own. She'd managed to keep her sister and Kim and everyone she loved out of Charlie's crosshairs. You don't run the first twenty-five miles of a marathon to send reinforcements in to finish the last mile. Even if that last mile feels like five hundred.

"I will do my job if it's the last damn thing I do," she said, and some days it felt like it would be. Like she'd be under his thumb until the day she died.

* * *

"Perfect."

Gayle rested her hands on Julia's shoulders, admiring her work in the mirror. "Want to see the back?"

"Hell yeah," Julia said, and Gayle swiveled her around and held up a silver hand mirror for her to use to see the French twist.

"I love it," she said, carefully touching the tendrils that fell on her neck.

"You do?"

"Of course! I love everything you do."

"Don't mess it up on the drive to the Presidio," Gayle said, wagging a finger playfully in admonishment, though she surely meant the directive too. Hair-styles were to be taken seriously.

"It's fifteen minutes away! What do you think I'm going to do? Hang my head out the limo window like a dog?"

"If you do that please make sure everyone knows I was not responsible for the mess. I only want credit for the good hair days," Gayle said.

"Thank you for coming in early for me on a Saturday to do this, when you're not even working," Julia said, gesturing to the empty salon. The front door was locked.

"Anything for you. Now I'll walk you out. And by the way, I want an update on your guy."

Her guy. Was Clay her guy? She didn't know what he was, except a sexy voice on the end of the phone. She'd gotten to know more about him in this last month from their easy chatter and conversations, and everything she learned made her long for him more. They never talked about a relationship. Never brought up seeing each other. Actual contact was off the table; they were only phone buddies.

But she didn't have time to fashion an answer to Gayle's question because when she opened the door to Fillmore Street, Skunk was pacing on the sidewalk like a big bored lion, walking back and forth in a zoo.

The hair on the back of her neck prickled in worry. Of all the days for Charlie to harass her. The bastard.

A sister's wedding day should be a sacred one. A day even Charlie could respect.

Gayle didn't notice him at first while she locked up. Then she turned around, and Skunk spoke to the hair-dresser.

"I was hoping I could get a haircut," he said gesturing to the salon with its pretty feminine windows decorated with silhouettes of women. This was clearly a salon catering mostly to the fairer sex, though Julia had seen a few men inside from time to time. They didn't look like Skunk, though. They weren't big beefy men with faces like slabs of meat, and ankle holsters holding guns. The men who walked through these doors were metrosexuals. Her eyes darted to his feet, and she saw the barest outline of his weapon. He never left home without it.

"We're closed now. Open again in an hour," Gayle said. "Someone will be here then to cut your hair."

"I'd really like one now," he said, then scrunched up his nose, squeezed shut his eyes, and covered his face with a hand as he sneezed so loudly it sounded like a honk. His forehead was sweaty, and he looked pale.

"I'm sure you do, sweetie, and ordinarily I'd open right up for you," she said in her best calm voice as she dipped a hand into her purse. She quickly found a tissue, and gave it to Skunk. He took it and muttered a *thanks*. "But I need to get some coffee in me, and if I don't my hands might be unsteady. So why don't you come back and someone else can take care of you then?"

He blew his nose, then rubbed the tissue across it. His eyes looked red and watery. "Or, maybe go home, take a hot bath and have some tea and come back tomorrow? You might be getting a nasty cold, honey."

"I think I have the flu," he said.

"Here." She reached in her pocket for a slip of paper and handed that to him. "A twenty percent off coupon, just for you. For when you're feeling better. You go get in bed and take care of that flu."

Skunk relented, nodding. "Thank you. I'll be back."

He lumbered away, and Julia had a sinking feel that *I'll be back* referred to something other than where he'd be an hour from now.

They were circling her, trying to trip her up however they could.

Charlie had sent this message—his sick way of letting her know he'd uncovered another soft spot of hers in her friendship with her stylist. His subtle, or not-so-subtle way of reminding her that he had no mercy. He was willing to do whatever it took to get his money by his deadline.

The deadline was looming ever closer.

* * *

Julia pet her sister's dog over and over, as if the animal might have a calming effect. Dogs sometimes did that, right? Settled nerves and made people happier.

She needed some of that right now, so she sat on the edge of the antique white couch stroking Ms. Pac-Man's soft fur, hoping it would turn these jitters inside her belly into a thing of the past.

She wasn't even the one walking down the aisle. She was the damn maid-of-honor and she was supposed to reassure the bride. But McKenna was ready, eager, and not a wink nervous, while all Julia could think about was the ticking clock. She'd texted Gayle a few times, ostensibly about her hair, but really to make sure her stylist was fine. Gayle was getting ready for an Arcade Fire concert, she'd said, so all was well.

Still, Julia couldn't help feeling as if someone was watching her. Waiting for her. Poised to take her down.

Focus on the bride.

Decked out in a vintage-style tea-length dress, McKenna applied her lip gloss then twirled once in front of the antique, gilded mirror in her suite at the swank Golden Gate Club in the Presidio, a coveted venue for weddings with its view of the San Francisco Bay and the Golden Gate Bridge.

"You look so beautiful, and this dress is so completely you," Julia said, even though she'd seen it many times. But that was her job—to shower the bride with extravagant compliments on her wedding day. It would also force her mind off the heightened state of panic inside her body.

"You're next, Jules," she said, and Julia scoffed.

She didn't even know how to respond. The notion of her being married was so foreign, her sister might as well be talking about orbiting Saturn right now. "Let's get you down the aisle," she said.

Julia washed her hands one final time. Yes, Ms. Pac-Man had had a pre-wedding bath, but even so she didn't want scent of a pooch on her as she held a bouquet. She grabbed her daisies, the perfect flowers for McKenna's sunny disposition, and held open the door for the other bridesmaids: McKenna's good friends Hayden and Erin, and Chris's sister, Jill, who had flown out from New York for the weekend, taking two days off from her starring role in the musical *Crash the Moon*.

They headed to the expansive grounds, across the rolling green hills, to the bluff overlooking the water. The waves lolled peacefully against the shore in the distance, and the afternoon sun warmed them. The weather gods were on their side today—the sky was a crystal blue, and there was no wind. A rare blessing in this windiest of cities, and Julia was grateful.

White chairs were spread across the lawn, and their friends and family were there. Julia spotted Davis in the second row, and instantly her thoughts flicked to Clay. The two men were best friends, and she found herself wondering if her name had ever come up in their conversations.

The music began and the other bridesmaids walked down the white runner spread out on the lawn. Julia turned to McKenna and whispered in her ear. "I love you. I'm so happy for you," she said, then she squeezed her hand.

"I love you too," McKenna said, and her voice threatened to break. Julia reached out, and gently wiped the start of a happy tear from her sister's eye. "Don't ruin your mascara."

"I won't."

Julia took her turn down the runner, thrilled to finally see this day arrive. Though it hadn't been a lengthy engagement—in fact it had been markedly short, clocking in at two mere months—this was a day that she'd longed to see. Nearly two years ago, the man McKenna had been involved with dumped her via voicemail twenty-four hours before their wedding, leaving her with a houseful of mixers, pasta makers and place settings she'd never use. Her sister had been devastated. Chris wasn't like that, not in the least, but Julia had asked a few days ago if she'd had any lingering worries.

"You nervous at all now that it's so close?"

"Nope. I've never been more sure of anything in my life," McKenna had said.

She looked it, too, radiant in her joy today.

When Julia reached the raised stage, her throat hitched, and a tear slipped down her cheek as she turned to watch McKenna walk down the aisle. She delighted at the song that filled the air. McKenna hadn't picked Pachelbel's Canon or the wedding march. She'd chosen hers and Chris's song—*Can't Help Falling in Love.*

That was the best kind of love, wasn't it? The kind where the love was its own entity, a living, breathing presence between two people, demanding to be felt. A life force of its own. That's what her sister and Chris had, and her heart soared with happiness that McKenna had found *the one.*

Chris couldn't take his eyes off his bride as he waited at the edge of the bluff, watching her every step as she walked closer. The last words of the Elvis song faded out as she stepped next to him. *Take my hand, take my whole life too.* He whispered something to her, and she whispered back, and Julia was no longer jam-packed with worries over Charlie and Skunk. It had all been replaced by this torrent of happiness she felt for the two of them.

As the justice of the peace cleared his throat, Julia quickly peeked at the crowd, spotting familiar faces—Chris's family, McKenna's videographer, her dog trainer, her friends from the fashion world, along with Chris's brother who stood next to him, some of his surfing buddies in the seats, and people he worked with on his TV show. Then her eyes landed on the profile of a handsome man in the back row who was taking a seat. A latecomer, he'd just arrived. The man raised his face and Julia's heart stopped with a quick shudder.

Then it started again when, somehow, across the crowd of people, the sea of suited men and elegantly-dressed women, of family and friends and new faces, he made eye contact with her, locking his gaze on hers. The sounds of the ceremony, of the vows being exchanged turned to white noise, and all she could see, hear, and feel was *him*. No longer separated by a continent. No longer connected only by the tether of email. He was one hundred feet away, and he never once stopped looking at her.

Her skin was hot, and her heart was beating loudly, and as soon as the groom kissed the bride and walked back down the aisle, she was damn near ready to launch herself into his arms.

CHAPTER SEVEN

Sometime in the last few weeks he'd decided several things.

That she might be lying. That she might be trouble. That he might be about to become the poster child for *fool me twice, shame on me.*

But most of all, he'd decided that his gut told him she'd meant what she said. Even though she hadn't given him the details of why there'd been a man with a gun demanding her presence, he'd made the choice to believe her.

Blind trust, maybe. Or possibly blind something else. Either way, his instincts said she was telling the truth. His gut had served him throughout his career, so he'd decided to listen to it.

Now that he was here with her, he wasn't thinking with his gut. He wasn't thinking at all. He was feeling.

His whole body was humming, vibrating at a frequency only she could sense. His skin sizzled, and blood rushed hot through his veins. Nearness to her was an aphrodisiac.

"I like your suit," she said, going first.

"I like your dress."

"You're here," she said with wonder in her voice as she eyed him up and down. He didn't think he'd ever tire of the way she looked at him with hunger, need, and passion.

"I'm here," he said, quirking up his lips. They stood gazing at each other, but they hadn't touched yet. They were inches apart, and there was something almost fragile about this moment. As if they might break if one of them moved. He didn't know who would make the first move, but he hoped it would be her since he'd made the effort to show up.

"How?" she asked, still breathless.

"Your sister and her husband."

"They invited you?" she asked, her lips curving into a wide, gorgeous smile.

"Invited. Or insisted. Take your pick."

"Really?" she asked, and a breeze blew by, making the soft little tendrils of her hair flutter against her neck. He wanted to bend his head to her neck, layer her skin in kisses that made her shiver in his arms and melt into him, that turned her so hot inside her knees went weak and she nearly buckled with desire. He'd catch her, hold her, make sure she didn't fall, except into him.

He did none of that. His hands were stuffed in his pockets, or else he'd be touching her, wrapping his arms around her, running his fingertips along her hipbone, covered in the fabric of her black dress.

"Yes. Really. Chris invited me a week ago, and said he needed his lawyer here. Which was about the worst case of acting I'd ever heard, since no one needs his entertainment lawyer at his wedding, so McKenna grabbed the phone, reprimanding him, and then laid it out."

"What did she say?"

"She said she thought it would make you happy if I were here, and that you being happy was the greatest gift she could have on her wedding day. Well, besides marrying Chris," he said with a happy shrug. "Far be it from me to deny the bride of my newest client her greatest wish."

He watched Julia process his words. She swallowed, drew in a sharp breath, and clasped her hand over her mouth, covering a sob. A tear slipped down her cheek.

Instantly, he reached for her, swiping the tear away and leaning in close. "You okay?"

She nodded. "I just love my sister so much," she said in a broken voice. "But she's wrong."

Clay stiffened. No. Not now. Not after he'd taken this big chance. This big leap. Not after all their emails and calls. "Why is she wrong?"

Julia shook her head. "Because I'm not just happy. I'm *unbelievably* happy that you're here."

The darkness lifted, and his entire body felt light and full of hope. She wrapped her arms around his neck, threading her fingers in his hair, and tilting her chin up to him. He ached all over just being near to her. She licked her lips, kept her eyes on him, and he'd never seen a more beautiful woman, nor had he ever wanted to kiss someone as much as he wanted to this very second.

He ran the backs of his fingers softly against her cheek, watching as she leaned into him, her eyes floating closed for a brief second as she whispered, "You may kiss the maid-of-honor."

"Now that makes me unbelievably happy," he said, gathering her in his arms, tugging her beautiful body close to his, and brushing his lips gently across hers. She gasped lightly when he made contact, that involuntary sound the most perfect reminder of why he'd listened to Chris and McKenna, snapped up a ticket, and flew across the country. Why he took the chance once again with Julia. He could pretend he was doing this for a client, simply responding properly to an invitation for a social occasion. He knew better than to lie to himself. He was doing this because he'd made the choice to trust her. The alternative—being without her—was too much to bear.

But he was also choosing to let go of the past. He wasn't going to blame Julia for Sabrina's problems, nor punish himself either by reassigning them to her. The month apart from her—all talk and no contact—had reset his head in some unexpected way, reassuring him that he could try again.

By God, how he wanted to try again as she melted into him, her body so tantalizingly close as they kissed under the sun, surrounded by wedding guests who surely didn't care what two random people were doing because they weren't the bride and the groom. They were the maid-of-honor and the man who *had* to have her, no matter the cost. He kissed her tenderly at first, light and soft as the moment called for, here on the bluff, San Francisco Bay waves rolling on by. But as she inched closer to him, pressing the full length of her gorgeous frame against his, the gentleness fell away. A groan worked its way up his chest. He pulled her harder, needing her as close as could be, needing her mouth. She whimpered and parted her lips, inviting him to taste more. He explored her with his tongue, kissing her the kind of way two lovers kiss when they haven't seen each other in a month.

What a long, hard month it had been. She wriggled her hips subtly against his cock, which was straining now against the zipper of his pants. The barest of contact with his erection sent his body spinning. "Julia," he whispered harshly, her name a warning.

Her mouth fell away from his, and she brushed her lips along his jaw, up to his ear. "I want you," she said, in a hot murmur. "I want you now."

Nothing else mattered but grabbing her hand, and finding the nearest coat closet so he could slam the door and take her.

But the second he laced his fingers through hers, someone tapped on her shoulder.

"Picture time!"

The bride was beaming, and her smile could light up a midnight skyline, he reckoned. But then, that's how it should be on your wedding day.

Julia brushed her hand once over the front of her dress, as if she were smoothing it out, then McKenna caught Clay's eye.

"You made it," she shrieked, then threw her arms around his neck. He angled himself so she couldn't feel his hard-on. The last thing he needed was the bride thinking he was a pervert, or telling the groom that his new lawyer had been sporting wood.

"Congratulations, McKenna. I'm so happy for you and Chris," he said, and when she pulled away he continued. "And I donated to the New York City ASPCA in your honor."

"Oh, you didn't have to," she said, then patted the outside of her leg, and a blond Lab-Hound-Husky arrived at her side, parking herself perfectly in a sit. "But Ms. Pac-Man thanks you."

"She's even cuter in person," Clay said, gesturing to the dog, before he extended a hand to the groom, congratulating him as well on the nuptials.

Soon, McKenna scurried her sister, her husband and her dog away for photos. Julia leaned in to give him a quick peck on the cheek before they headed to the bluff for a round of pictures.

Clay took a deep breath, and hoped the photographer made quick work behind the lens.

"Fancy meeting you here."

Clay turned to see his buddy Davis. "Hey man," he said, clapping his friend on the back, though Davis was joking—Clay had told him the other night that he'd be at the wedding. Davis was here with Jill, the groom's sister.

"Guess we're the odd men out," Davis said, tipping his forehead to the wedding party that included the women both of them were involved with.

Wait. Was he involved with Julia again? Or was it crazy to think that, given the track record they both had of running? He didn't know what they were, or what they would be.

"Yep. Looks like we are," Clay said. "Think this'll be you anytime soon?"

Davis nodded, a sneaky glint in his eyes. "As a matter of fact, I believe I will be popping the question at the Tony Awards next month."

Clay smiled widely, then hugged his friend. "Congrats, man. That's fantastic. You two are great together."

"I think so too."

As he chatted with Davis, neither of them did a very good job of looking anywhere but at the wedding party, Davis's eyes on Jill, Clay's on Julia. There was something both peaceful and right about this moment, this wedding, these people he barely knew who'd invited him into their most important day. It felt fitting to be here, and soon the gorgeous redhead would be back by his side where she belonged.

* * *

There was no time for a quickie. The moment the photographer had finished shooting the wedding party, the cocktail hour started, as waiters passed out flutes of bubbly champagne. The festivities had moved inside to a gorgeous reception room with a baby grand piano and floor-to-ceiling glass windows overlooking the water. The decor reflected the bride's and groom's passion for games and animals with the name cards at place settings stamped with Mr. Monopoly, and the centerpiece flowers boasting a wooden cutout of a hound dog.

Chris tapped a fork against a glass, cleared his throat and stood next to his new wife by the head table. "First of all, thank you so much for coming. I'm pretty sure I'm the luckiest guy in the world simply because I have this woman as my wife. To also see so many friends and family here makes the occasion all the better, even though I'd have married her anywhere—in a box, on a boat, in the rain, on a train," he said, then paused to look at McKenna. She rolled her eyes playfully. "What? It's true," he said to her, but loud enough for everyone to hear. He faced the guests again. "Anyway, I'm going to keep this short and sweet, and turn the microphone over to the best man and the maid-of-honor. And since I'm a ladies first kind of a guy, we'll start with Julia. Take it away."

Julia crossed the few feet to Chris and took the microphone, then turned to the crowd. "It's truly an honor to be here and to be able to say a few words about my favorite person in the world and *her* favorite person in the world," she said, stopping to gesture at Chris.

"Hey! You're still a favorite," McKenna called out.

Julia waved her off playfully. "I'm still a little surprised though as to why Chaucer isn't here to give a toast. Do you all know Chaucer?" she asked the crowd. Most of them shook their heads. "Let me tell you a story. Chaucer is our friend's Siamese cat, and he was something of a matchmaker for Chris and McKenna. He's one of those dastardly Siamese cats who likes to make his mark in the world. But, lest everyone think cat pee is a bad thing all the time, there are the rare cases where cat pee brings two people together. Because when Chaucer peed on McKenna's camera many months ago, she brought it to the electronics store to find a replacement. And who would she happen to meet there but this man," Julia said patting Chris on the shoulder. "And Chris, being an industrious and resourceful fellow, and naturally, being completely smitten with McKenna from the second he saw her, gamely offered to repair her camera," she said, a smile breaking across her face as she told the story. From across the crowd of glittering lights and gorgeously arrayed tables, she spotted Clay, his eyes fixed on her. Suddenly she felt as if the whole room had disappeared and she was talking only to him. Sharing a love story with her man. "Of course, it wasn't always easy, and McKenna had a bit of a stubborn side about some things."

"I'll say," Chris chimed in, as he draped an arm around his wife and planted a sweet kiss on her cheek, earning a collective *aww* from the guests.

"But here we are, despite the stubbornness from my big sis, because she realized what a good thing she had in front of her, and that giving up her stubborn ways was worth it." She locked eyes with Clay once more, and the lightness of the speech drained away, replaced instead by the deeper possibility of whether she could give up the things she held too tightly. She'd never truly considered it until that moment, but was there a chance she was being stubborn, too, by clutching her secrets and her shame in her hands? She'd always considered her troubles to be completely solo problems, but they were growing far less solitary given Charlie's encroachment on her personal territory lately, from his heated asides about McKenna to sending his heavy with the runny nose to her salon that morning.

But she didn't want to think about Skunk or any of them right now. She wouldn't let them mar this day.

With a quick swallow, she soldiered on. "And, as anyone can see, they are perfect for each other, from their shared love of karaoke, to their steadfast belief that California is the *only* suitable place to live, to their affection for games, from Candyland all the way to Halo and Qbert. Because ultimately, isn't that part and parcel of what makes a love last through the years? Common interests and passion, whether it's for adventure," she said, and now she was talking *only* to the man across the room, "or a good crime flick. Or even just the same, how shall we say, *preferences*," she said, taking a beat to enjoy the way he fought back a naughty grin. "I like to think those little things are also big things. And Chris and McKenna have all of that. So, here's to the bride and groom." She held up her champagne glass.

As Chris's brother began his toast seconds later, she threaded her way through the guests and clinked glasses with Clay. "Cheers."

"That was a beautiful speech," he said, his deep brown eyes searching hers.

"I meant every word."

"Every word?" He raised an eyebrow as he took a drink.

"Every single one."

* * *

After the first dance, McKenna tugged her friends to the floor when Jill belted out a karaoke version of Matchbox Twenty's "Overjoyed." Julia felt the soprano's voice literally vibrate through the reception hall, her Broadway belt glittering with energy and strength as she wowed the crowd. "She's totally going to win a Tony for Best Actress in a Musical, isn't she?" Julia said to Clay, with chills on her arms as a result of Jill's talent.

"Honestly, I don't see how she can't. She brings down the house every single night in *Crash the Moon.*"

Once Jill stepped off the stage, the music shifted back to the sound system and Billie Holiday's jazzy voice warbled through the speakers. "My sister loves the old standards. Sinatra, Holiday, the King," she said by way of explanation.

"As do I," he said, taking her hand and leading her to the dance floor as "All or Nothing At All" piped overhead.

Clay's hands found their way to her hips, settling in comfortably as she roped her arms around his neck, her fingertips brushing against his soft, thick hair. The song played as other couples danced, and they swayed past Jill and Davis, and Chris and McKenna. Julia kept her gaze on Clay, loving the intensity in his eyes. "I'm glad you're here," she said, because it felt so much better to be patently honest with him than to deny what she felt. She'd flopped back and forth between shooing her feelings out the door and acting upon them. She didn't want the back and forth anymore.

"So am I."

They twirled in lazy circles, as the words and music filled the room.

"*All or nothing at all. Half a love never appealed to me. If your heart never could yield to me then I'd rather have nothing at all.*"

The words pulsed around Julia like living, breathing creatures, then slipped into all the crevices of her hardened heart. They reminded her that halfway was the worst way. She'd tried so desperately to pack herself in ice, to feel *nothing* at all those nights at Charlie's games, but instead she'd felt everything. She felt the shame of Dillon's betrayal, the anger at being Charlie's pawn, and the cruel distance she had kept with the man she was falling for. She'd always thought she was protecting her family and friends by keeping her own secrets, but the events of this morning outside the salon were a cold reminder that blindfolding them to her problems might not work forever. Whether she liked it or not, she might very well need help. Clay had offered to listen, to sort through things. She knew he couldn't snap a finger and make her debt magically disappear, but maybe he could at least be there for her as she raced to meet Charlie's moving target of a deadline.

"Clay," she began nervously, and already she could hear the potholes in her own voice. She'd have an easier time speaking with marbles in her mouth than saying *this.*

"Yes?" he asked, tugging her closer, warming her skin with his body.

All or nothing at all. If it's love there is no in-between.

Billie Holiday whispered in her ear, urging her on, reminding her to be strong. "You know when you asked me that night at my apartment what was going on?"

"Yes," he said, like a gentle invitation for her to keep speaking. She could do this. She could tell him. After all, he'd flown all the way across the country. He'd opened his heart to her, taking chances left and right that she'd barely earned. He wanted her honesty more than anything else, and though she might scare him all the way back to New York when she told him, she also knew he wasn't a man who trafficked in fear. This man could take on anyone.

"I'm ready to tell you," she said, the words tumbling on top of each other, jostling to break free.

"Tell me," he said, gripping her hips harder as his eyes widened. He stopped dancing, grasped her hand, and guided her outside of the reception hall.

Once outside, she shivered. The evening had settled in, bringing with it the California chill from the bay. He took off his suit jacket, and slipped it over her shoulders. The gesture emboldened her.

"You remember that guy who came up to me out-side my apartment?" Her stomach nosedived as she began. "When I lied about who you were?"

"Yes. Of course."

She inhaled sharply, letting the cool air fill her chest, hoping it would settle her flip-flopping insides. "I lied because I was scared. Because I was trying to protect you. Which I know sounds silly, because you're this big, strong man," she said, reaching out to touch his arm lightly. "But I don't want him or anyone going after you because I care about you."

"Why would he or anyone go after me?"

This was the hardest part. When she told him *why*. The words threatened to lodge in her chest, refusing to come out, but she shucked off the red-hot shame. "My ex? The one who's gone—I told you about him that night in your bath?"

His features tightened, and his brow furrowed. "Yeah. Where is he?"

"I still don't know. The IRS is looking for him, and I haven't a clue. He left the country, and he left with $100,000 stolen from the mob. He claimed the money was a loan for me to expand my bar, so when he took off, the mob boss came to collect. With me."

Clay's mouth hung open.

She never thought this polished, confident man would be speechless, but that's what she'd done to him because he'd gone mute from the shock. Seconds ticked by, then a full minute, it seemed. He scrubbed a hand across his jaw as if he were thinking, trying to process what she'd said.

"I know it's probably not something you hear too often. *Hi, sweetie. I'm wanted by the mob.*"

"No," he said, managing a brief, dry laugh. "Don't hear that very often at all."

"So when Stevie came by he needed me to go to a game."

"Game?"

"I play poker for this guy, Charlie. Stevie is his enforcer. I'm Charlie's ringer. He makes me play in rigged poker games to win back the money Dillon stole."

Clay stepped away, looking unsteady on his feet and ashen. "Are you serious?"

She nodded. "Completely. I'm really amazingly good at poker. Always have been. And I win most of the time. And now I hate playing because I'm forced to play for him to pay off a debt that isn't even mine."

"That's a fucking mess, Julia," he said, his voice a raw scrape. And it scared her.

He was going to run now, wasn't he? Nobody wanted this kind of mess in their lives. He probably didn't believe her, either. Probably thought she was lying to him like Sabrina had done, and figured she was going to ask him for money too. Crap. She had to fix this.

She moved closer. "Did I scare you off?"

"No. I'm just . . . I just . . . I didn't think that was the issue."

"What did you think it was?"

"I honestly don't know. But that's some crazy stuff, Julia," he said, and she detected a note of skepticism.

She cycled through things to do or say to prove herself. "I want you to trust me and I know you have every reason not to trust me. You also have to know I'm not asking you for money. I've never asked anyone for money. If I were going to I would ask my sister, but I have kept her and everyone I love out of this because it's my problem. I want you to believe me. Do you believe me?"

His lips parted and he paused briefly then said yes. But she needed him to believe it with every ounce of his being.

"No. I want you to believe me with the same certainty that you want to fuck me," she said, pushing hard on his chest now. Flames of anger licked her chest. She'd opened her deepest, darkest secret and she didn't want a shred of doubt.

He held up his hands as if he were backing off from her. "Fine. I believe you."

"The expression in your eyes tells me otherwise. You asked me to open up to you. I'm baring my fucking heart to you. Charlie gave me a deadline, and he's threatening my bar and my co-worker, and he showed up this morning at my hair salon, and he's circling me," she said, holding her hands out wide. She flashed onto something he'd told her once about a friend of his. "I am mad and I am terrified. I'm not asking you for money. I'm asking you to believe me, and you need to believe me completely. So call your friend."

He crinkled his nose as if her words didn't compute. "My friend?"

"The lawyer who runs people down for you? You said he tracked down intel on people you weren't sure about."

"Yeah, my friend Cam. He can get the goods on anyone."

Julia dug into her small satin clutch purse and grabbed her phone. She thrust it at him. "Call him. The guy is Charlie Stravinski, he owns Mr. Pong's restaurant in China Town," she said, rattling off the address. "He also owns Charlie's Limos. I'm sure your friend can verify who he is. That's the guy who owns me."

"Julia," he said softly, his voice strained, and that sound was terribly familiar. It felt lethal. It was the sound of his voice when he ran. It was the way he'd spoken to her on the street. She tensed all over, and she wished she could unwind the last fifteen minutes of honesty, zip them up and toss them in a body bag into the ocean. She should have continued leaving him in the blissfully ignorant state that made him jet out to San Francisco to see her. He'd been falling for her; she could see it, feel it, sense it. Now she'd shattered what they could have had. Whoever said honesty was the best policy didn't have the mob on her tail.

He breathed out hard, pressed his lips together, and seemed to be debating. "Julia," he said again, his expression softer. "You don't have to prove it. I came out here because I trust you, and if we're going to be together the way we want, the way I want, the way you want, I'm not going to ask you to prove who some guy is."

But she needed him to know she wasn't making up Charlie. "It's important to me that you know this for certain and not just because I said so. I need to have proven myself to you. Call your friend, give him the info, and you'll know I'm not lying. I have a price tag on my head."

CHAPTER EIGHT

It was almost too crazy to believe, but the truth was messy. Lies were ironclad. They added up too neatly. Lies were padded so thick they became airtight and couldn't breathe. The truth was frayed, like the tattered end of a rope. The truth was full of holes that were evidence of its veracity. Still, he could tell proof was vitally important to her, so he pulled his own phone from his pocket and dialed Cam.

"Hey man, can you run a quick check on someone for me?"

"Abso-fucking-lutely for you," his friend said in his gregarious voice.

Clay gave him the basic details. "Just let me know what kind of business he's running. Doable?"

"This is easy. I'm in front of my laptop right now, and will run a few quick searches. That is, if my lady friend doesn't come back and try to distract me."

Clay smiled briefly. "Have fun with Tess. But take care of me too."

"You bastard, you owe me so much. I love it when you owe me. I love running down shit for you because it gives me one more thing to add to my totals. There's only one other person I do this for free for," Cam said, his voice stretching across the country like a big old Texas-style hug.

"Who's that?"

"I'm not saying but she's a lot prettier than you."

"I should hope so."

He hung up, and returned to Julia. She looked different than she had before. She'd always been tough, strong, a woman of the world. Now she looked empty, as if she'd shed all her emotions and replaced them with cool blankness. He reached for her, gripping her arms gently but firmly as he kept his eyes fixed on her. "That story is crazy, and I hate what he did to you and I hate that anyone wants to hurt you, and here's the thing—I won't let them now. You know that, right? You're with me, and that means I'm here to help you. You tried to protect me and that was the most adorable, sweetest, sexiest thing anyone has ever done, but you don't have to because that's my job. Got that?"

She said nothing, just stared hard at him. She was shutting down, and he was having none of that. Not after she'd finally opened up. "I'm not running," he said firmly, refusing to let her look away. "I'm here for you. I'm here with you, and I want to help you. That's what I do. That's what I want to do for you."

"Why?" She crossed her arms over her chest.

"Why?" he said, his voice louder. He was going to have to make this abundantly clear. "Because I flew here to see you. Because you are under my skin. Because this fucking bastard left you with a shit ton of problems and if I ever find him I will make sure he pays. And because you have the mafia after you."

"That doesn't scare you? Make you want to run?" She shot him a challenging stare, almost as if she were daring him to walk away.

"No," he said crisply.

There wasn't a chance in hell that was happening. He straightened his spine, planted his feet wide, making it clear in every way that he was staying. "It makes me want to stay."

"Why do you want to help me?"

He shook his head in frustration, but deep down he understood why she was behaving like this. She'd admitted something terribly private, and self-preservation was familiar ground for her.

"May I remind you of your toast in there?" He tipped his chin to the reception. Through the glass, the guests were still spinning on the dance floor, the twinkling lights illuminating their steps. Waiters moved nimbly about, passing out appetizers. "Common interests and passion? Ring a bell?" he said, waiting for her to acknowledge what she'd said a mere hour ago. She nodded once. "I feel the same."

She didn't answer him, so he reached for her hands, unpeeled them from her chest, and drew them behind her back.

"Now, don't go cold on me. If you do, I will have to tie your hands the next time I fuck you," he said, fixing her with an intensely serious look.

Her lips quirked up, as if she were trying hard to hold in a smile. "That's a promise, gorgeous," he added.

"But that's a promise I like," she whispered, and her words were a straight shot to his groin. They had to have set some kind of record for most hours being near each other without tearing off clothes. He pressed his hips against hers, holding her in place, watching her eyes go hazy as she felt him.

"Now listen. I made the phone call you asked me to make. I don't care right now about what Cam is doing, or finding out, or anything. I care about you, woman. And I haven't fucked you in a month, so if I were you I'd be thinking about how you're going to spend the rest of the reception without any underwear on because it's about to come off."

"Is that a promise too?" she asked, and the playfulness he knew and longed for had returned to her voice.

"Yes. Now I'm going to deliver on it." He grabbed her hand and linked his fingers through hers, guiding her across the lawn, past the reception hall, and to a back door that led down a carpeted hallway. This was the kind of place that had swank bathrooms, and that was what he needed right now. He walked quickly, scanning the area for an opening. When he spotted a bathroom, he knocked once, opened the elegant white door, and locked it quickly behind them.

The bathroom was small with marble floors and a sink that had just enough room for Julia to perch on. He lifted her up onto the edge of the vanity.

She was trembling.

Concern sliced through him. He lifted her chin gently. "You okay?"

She nodded, but didn't speak.

"Julia, what is it?"

She shook her head, and seemed to swallow back a tear. "I'm sorry, I'm just super emotional today."

He leaned into her, resting his forehead against hers. "It's okay to be emotional. Your sister got married, and you shared something intense with me."

She reached her arms around his waist, her hands gripping the back of his white shirt. She still wore his suit coat and looked unbelievably hot in it. "And I want you to make love to me right now," she said in a breathless voice, her cheek pressed against his.

"Then I will make love to you," he said, bringing his hands to her face. He cupped her cheeks, and raised her chin so she met his eyes. "You're so fucking beautiful," he said, the words spilling out without control. He had to say it, had to tell her over and over.

"So are you," she said, and ran her hands down the buttons on his shirt, her fingers reaching his waistband. She unhooked his belt, then in seconds she was unzipping him, reaching a hand into his briefs.

His head fell back when she touched his cock for the first time in a month. He groaned as her soft, nimble fingers gripped him. She stroked him up and down, and he could almost stay like this because the feel of her hand on him was like a quick dive into a zone of white-hot pleasure. He rocked into her hand, and she gripped him tighter, making a fist that felt so fucking good wrapped around him.

Far too good.

Somehow, the part of his brain that wasn't drugged out on her sent a message to his hand, and he wrapped it around hers, making her stop. He shook his head, narrowing his eyes at her. "Now, Julia. You're not playing fair, and when you don't play fair, it means I'm going to have to take matters into my hands."

"What do you mean?"

"It means," he said, sliding off his belt, watching her eyes widen with lust as he dangled it in front of her, "that you're wearing this."

A wicked grin played across her lips and she wriggled closer. "Where?" she said breathily and he loved how she went with it. She didn't freak out. She *wanted* this kind of play. With his free hand he traced a line down her cheek, savoring her reaction as she shivered, leaning her face into his touch.

"Your hands," he said, reaching for them and placing a kiss on the inside of each of her wrists before he ran the leather along the outside, wrapping it around once, twice, and carefully pulling the end through the buckle. He gave it a good tug to make sure it was secure, but not so tight that the leather would dig into her skin.

"Now what?" she asked, holding out her bound hands in front of her.

"Now this," he said, gently pushing up the fabric of her dress, inch by inch, revealing more of her delicious skin. When he reached the apex of her thighs, he breathed in deep as a bolt of lust slammed into his body. "Keep your hands in your lap, Julia. Don't move them," he said, and kneeled down in front of her. "Do you understand?"

"Yes."

"Don't move your hands at all."

"I won't," she said, and her soft voice was a promise.

"Open your legs for me."

She parted her legs wider, spreading open for him as she sat perched on the sink, her immobile hands against her belly. He pushed the skirt to her waist, and ran his nose along the outside of her underwear, inhaling her, and letting her flood his senses completely. She gasped sharply. The sound of her pleasure tore through him like electricity.

He looked up at her to see her eyes floating shut. "Watch me," he commanded, gripping her thighs in his hands. "Watch me as I make you come with your panties on."

"What are you going to do to me?" she asked breathily.

"I just said what I'm going to do to you. Did you think I was joking?"

She shook her head, and he flicked his tongue across the panel of her panties, wet already with her heat. "I can taste you even with your underwear on," he murmured, his mouth against her. "I can make you shudder and writhe without even touching your pussy."

She moaned, a desperately needy whimper of desire. "You can. Yes, you can."

"You are so hot for me right now, aren't you?" he said, flicking his tongue against the swollen outline of her clit. She cried out a *yes,* and tried grabbing at his hair with her tied-up hands, managing to brush a few strands. He looked up at her. "Let me," he growled. "Let me control your pleasure."

He returned his mouth to her legs, tasting her once more through the cotton. She was so wet her panties were soaked through. The scent of her arousal washed over him, desire coursing thickly through his veins. He pressed his hands on the inside of her thighs, spreading her wider, lavishing fast, quick flicks against her wet center. It was as if the scrap of fabric was no longer there. He could taste her juices on his tongue, her desire so intense that she cried out loudly with every touch. Panting hard, she tried to grab at his hair again. He gently swatted her hands away. "Let go," he said roughly. "Let go so I can bring you there."

"Bring me there, Clay," she groaned as she wriggled her hips into his face, trying to get closer to the source of her pleasure. "Please bring me there."

"I will, gorgeous. I always will," he said, his lips returning to her wet pussy that tasted so delicious even with her underwear still on. He reached his hands underneath her ass, holding onto her cheeks as he pressed his tongue harder against her clit, licking, kissing, tasting until she bucked against his mouth.

She cried out, her mouth falling open, her eyes squeezed shut, her body writhing into him.

Once her movements slowed, he rose and pulled off her panties, and brought them to his nose. "You smell so fucking good," he said, then stuffed them into his pocket. "These truly are useless now."

Her lips rose in a sweet smile. "What if you turn me on again? And I walk around the reception hot and dripping between my legs?"

He buzzed his lips against the column of her neck, traveling up to her ear. "Then tell me and I will slide my hand up your legs, coat my fingers in your wetness and suck it off."

She breathed out hard, her reaction telling him she liked his idea.

"Now, I believe you wanted me to make love to you?"

She nodded, biting gently down on her lip. "So badly."

"I'm going to," he said, stroking her cheek, then running his fingers along the smooth skin of her collarbone. "And I want you to know that all this time I've been fucking you and making love to you. But this time, I'm only making love to you."

"That's what I want right now from you. That's all I want," she said, her voice layered with honesty and need as she leaned her face into his hand. Then held up her wrists in front of him. "But what about this?"

* * *

"Put your hands around my neck," he instructed.

She shot him a quizzical look as she raised her bound hands. He offered his head, letting her slide her hands behind his neck. "Like that?"

"Yes. Now you can't let go of me as I make love to you," he told her as he reached inside his briefs, and freed his erection once more.

"But I don't want to let go of you," she said, and she felt like a new woman being able to say these things to him, speaking so freely, even if it was about sex. Saying all those other things, as hard and as harrowing as it had been, had lifted a terrible weight from her shoulders, and now she experienced a freedom she hadn't known in a long time. She could say what she felt and not be afraid. And she could tell from the look in his eyes, so tender and hungry too, that he loved this side of her.

"Good. That's how I want you to feel," he said as he gripped his cock, and rubbed the head against her wet folds. She cried out again in pleasure.

"I want you so badly, Clay. *Please.*"

"I know you do," he said, dragging his hard length along her. She wanted him to know how much she trusted him with everything. In this moment she was trusting him with her pleasure, so she opened her legs more.

"I'm yours," she whispered, holding his gaze. "Take me how you want me."

He breathed out hard, her words of submission clearly sending him soaring. "You are mine," he said, his voice rough, but his touch so tender, as he slowly pushed inside her.

"Oh God," she whimpered. "You feel so good."

"It's been too long," he said, but still he took his time entering her, and she savored it, the feeling of being filled inch by delicious inch. He was so hard and so thick, and she could feel him stretching her once more.

"I don't want to go without you again," she whispered.

"Don't go without me." He buried himself in her, holding on hard to her hips as he sank deeper. She couldn't move. She was under his control, from him holding her hips, to her hands locked around his head, but he took care of her, thrusting in that deliciously tantalizing way he had, rolling his hips, taking his time.

He rocked into her, and she moved with him, hitting an exquisite synch. He groaned against her neck, pushing the strap of her dress down her arm. "I love it like this," he said, brushing his lips along her naked shoulder.

"Why do you like me tied up sometimes?"

"Because." He cupped the back of her head in a strong hand. "Because the way I feel for you is so out of control that this is one way for me to feel in control again," he said, his voice a low rasp in her ear.

She shuddered from his words. "Then control me," she whispered, arching her back, showing him that she could give in to this need he had. "Because," she began, echoing his word as hot molten sparks shot through her body, "I love everything you do to me."

"And do you love this?" he said, holding on tight, driving into her so she could feel him deep and hard inside her. "You like when I make love to you like this? Because that's what I'm doing right now."

"I know," she said breathlessly, and after a night of revealing her secrets, she could no longer keep the truth hidden. "You are, and I love it because I feel everything. I feel everything for you," she said, coming as close to saying those three words as she could.

He hitched in a breath. "God, Julia. I feel everything for you. Every single thing. And I want your pleasure again. I want to feel you come on me. Show me that I can do this to you over and over, and make you feel everything."

Pleasure spun through her body on a wild ride, racing through every corner, touching down in her belly, in her breasts, along her thighs. Even in her toes. "You can do anything to me," she cried out, as she felt herself reaching the brink. She tightened her arms around him trying to tug him as close as he could be. He held onto her, his cock buried inside of her, his lovemaking touching her so deep with its intensity that she was in another world, another realm, where she was bathed solely in the never-ending bliss of a climax that promised to rocket through her body.

Her head leaning back, her mouth falling open, she tried desperately to keep her noises to a minimum but it was futile as waves of pleasure slammed into her, and she came hard on him. He followed her there, his body shuddering, his chest heaving, as he thrust one final time. She felt as if she could never be close enough to him.

Never.

"I'm going to help you," he said, his voice strong as he promised her something she knew would be tough to give. "This is a promise. I'm going to find a way to help you out of this, and then I'm going to find your ex."

She didn't know that he could do either, but the fact that he wanted to was one more reason to fall into him.

CHAPTER NINE

The bride sat on the groom's lap, and his arms were wrapped around her waist. Julia held a glass of champagne and laughed at something Chris said. Jill reached across to punch Chris on the shoulder, and he rubbed the spot where she swatted him, clearly pretending it hurt. Then they all laughed, and Clay made up the words they were saying in his head.

He stood outside, watching the reception unfold through the windows. His phone was pressed to his ear.

"So what did you learn?"

"That Charlie Stravinski loves greenbacks more than anything in the world," Cam said.

"How so?" Clay turned away from the scene, and walked down the hill.

"He's got his fingers in all sorts of pies. He runs this limo company, right? Charlie's Limos. Totally legit, but it's his Bada Bing," Cam said.

"The strip club in *The Sopranos*."

"Yep. It's a clean business, and everything flows under that. He's got the market locked up in San Fran on sports betting. That's his big cash cow. He does concert tickets too—steals them and resells them at scalper prices. His growth market, though, is in poker. He runs a lot of big executive games in the Valley. He just started running some games in New York too," Cam said, and Clay stopped at a tree, setting his palm against the trunk.

"He's working out of the Big Apple now?"

"Seems he is. And he's a big-ass loan shark too."

"Oh well, of course," Clay said sarcastically, because Charlie was growing more conniving with every new detail. "Did you get the story behind Mr. Pong's?"

"You bet your ass I did. Used to belong to good old Mr. Pong himself. But Mr. Pong needed money to pay off an investment that went belly up, so Charlie loaned him the dough, putting up his restaurant as collateral."

"Let me guess. He never came up with the money."

"Bingo," he said enunciating every syllable. "Charlie took over, and word on the street is Mr. Pong is living on the street."

"He's homeless?" Clay said, his voice thick with shock.

"That's what I hear. His restaurant was all he had, and it's all Stravinski's now. Tons of VCs in the city eat there. Charlie runs his games above the restaurant and he has lunch there every day at twelve-thirty. Those fuckers love their routines, don't they?"

He steeled himself for the next question. "What about drugs?"

"Nope. He's as squeaky clean as they come in that regard. But . . ." Cam said, his voice trailing off into a territory that Clay wasn't so sure he wanted to go. But he had to.

"But what?" he asked wearily, as a cold gust of wind snapped. The night cooled off quickly by the bay.

"My sources say he might be making a move into the world's oldest profession, so there's that."

Clay clenched a fist, his fingers digging hard into his palm. He could slam it against the tree, bang it hard and unleash this coiled ball of anger eating up his chest, but that wouldn't do him a lick of good. He gritted his teeth, and turned away from his temptation.

"'Course, if it were up to me, I'd advise him to stay out of that racket," Cam continued.

"Thanks for looking into all that, man," he said. Then he stopped in his tracks. "Wait. There's someone else I need you to look into."

"Who's that?"

But Clay didn't know Dillon's last name. "I need to get more info. Let me get back to you on that."

"You know where to find me. And I'll see you Saturday for our game?"

Clay nodded. "I'll be there," he said, and as soon as the words were spoken, something started to click.

He ended the call, but he didn't head back inside. Instead, he watched from a distance, rubbing a hand across his jaw as he began to hatch a plan.

* * *

A few glasses of champagne later, Julia was feeling like the drink herself—bubbly and effervescent. Though that might simply be due to the gorgeous man with his arm draped possessively around her. He'd been by her side since he returned from making his phone call, and she loved that he found ways to touch her all night, whether he brushed her fingertips *accidentally* when he took her glass to refill, or when he absently traced a soft line along her hipbone as the cake was being served.

Having him here with her almost made her forget about the troubles that awaited her. He had that effect, as if he were a magic elixir that erased all the bad. Or maybe that was the magic of falling, the way it was the ideal blend of intoxication, and could blot out all but the tingling in her shoulders, the flip in her belly, the thump of her heart when he looked at her. His gaze was filled with intensity and passion, with desire and tenderness. That was how his eyes roamed her as he held open the door to a taxi after they'd said goodbye to the few remaining guests, the bride and groom having been sent on their way already.

The second the door closed, she leaned into him and sighed happily as she grazed her fingers along his collar. "You're coming home with me," she said.

"That I am, gorgeous. That I am," he said, and removed her hand from his shirt. She shot him a curious look as he knotted his fingers through hers. The cab sped out of the parking lot and down the twisty, hilly roads. He grasped her hand harder as if he were about to make a point. "I have a plan."

"Already?" she said, arching an eyebrow.

He brushed a finger against that taunting eyebrow, sending it back into place. "Yes, already. What do you think clients pay me the big bucks for? To sit on my ass and not think quickly?"

She laughed. "Fine. You got me there. But let me make one thing clear, Mr. Big Bucks, you are not paying it off for me."

He held up his hands as if in surrender.

"You were going to try to, weren't you?"

"Actually no," he said firmly.

"Because there's no way I'm taking it. I haven't asked anyone for money. I meant what I said—if I were going to ask for help, McKenna would be the first person I'd turn to, and I haven't breathed a word to her, so don't even think about it."

"You considering letting me get a word in edgewise?" he asked as the cab slowed to a stop at a light.

"Maybe. But if you even think about offering, I will do this," she said, putting her hands over her ears and singing, "La la la, I am not listening."

He pulled her hands off her ears. "You think I don't know you? You think I don't listen? That I can't figure out already from knowing you the way I do that you'd never ever take money from me or another man?"

She narrowed her eyes at him playfully. The fizzy effect of the champagne was still rolling through her bloodstream.

"I know you, woman," he continued. "You are independent and stubborn and fiery. Give me some goddamn credit. I would not make you an offer I know you'd walk away from."

"Ooh, you're going to make me an offer," she said, tap dancing her fingertips along his arm. "I. Can't. Wait."

He rolled his eyes. "You are red-hot trouble."

"Tell me about it," she fired back. "And now you know exactly how much trouble you have gotten yourself into," she said and laughed, the kind that vibrated through her whole body and made her clutch her belly. It felt so damn good, because she hadn't laughed about her situation in ages. Never, come to think about it. Now she could because she was no longer in it alone.

"And yet, I'm not walking away, am I?" He grabbed hold of her arms and pulled her close for a hard, fierce kiss that made her feel giddy and wanted at the same time. She was no longer living with armor on. She'd shucked off the heavy metal layers, making herself vulnerable, but lighter too. Something that felt disturbingly like joy raced through her veins as they kissed, and though their kisses had always rattled and hummed like a rock concert, this one was poetry too. It was bliss and beauty as the world shined bright in her heart.

She wasn't finished with Charlie; but for the first time, she could see a way through because she had a teammate.

She broke the kiss as the cab turned a corner into her neighborhood, and still she was smiling. She wanted to know Clay's plan, but she was also enjoying this newfound freedom from releasing all her own secrets she'd clutched tightly to her chest. "No, you're not walking away. You're driving away with me. Like we're in a getaway car. Or cab, really," she said, gesturing to the driver.

He shook his head, clapped his hand down on her thigh. "Let's focus now, Julia. You know how you said Charlie took the fun out of playing? How he perverted your love of the game?"

She nodded. "Yep. He sure did."

"I know how to get it back," he said, as the cab swerved around a bus onto her street. She jerked sideways, her shoulder bumping hard against his.

"Ouch," she said, rubbing her shoulder.

"You okay?"

She nodded. "You just have a really hard shoulder."

The car pulled up to the curb. "Hard shoulders are good things," he said, and reached for his wallet. "I got this."

"Thank you," she said, and opened the door and stepped out of the cab. She lifted her face to the night sky, breathing in the cool air and the starlight until she heard a voice.

"Hey."

She swiveled around and saw Max stalking towards her from the front stoop of her apartment. Tension roared back into her body in a heartbeat as Skunk's goon-in-training with the baby face and the barrel body stared coldly at her. She glanced over at the cab where Clay was busy handing the driver a credit card.

"Charlie sent me to find you."

"It's Saturday. I'm not playing tonight."

"Yeah, but he wants you to know you're going to New York next weekend for a game. He has some new blood in the city from the startups there, and he wants you to hustle them."

She straightened her spine, liquid courage coursing through her. "What if I don't want to?"

His eyes widened with anger, and in seconds his hand was on the back of her neck. "You think you can talk to me that way?"

He grappled at her skin, digging in. She swatted at his arm, trying to knock him away, but he was more than double her size. "Let go of me," she spat out.

"Let go of her," Clay said in a cool, cold voice.

Max shifted his focus to Clay, who was now by her side. "Who the fuck are you?"

"I'm the guy who's going to make you let go of her," he said, and before Julia could process what was happening his elbow came down hard on Max's arm, freeing her from his grip. Then Clay's fist connected with Max's jawline with a loud crunch. Julia cringed, the sharp snap echoing down the street.

Max grunted, his eyes nearly popping out from surprise. His gaze darted down at his ankle, and fear flashed hard and fast before her eyes. Oh God, did he have a gun?

"No!" she screamed, but the sound was cut short when Clay slammed a fist into Max's belly, and the man unleashed a loud grunt as he doubled over. He was fast for his size though, and quickly straightened up. Clay cocked his fist to swing again, but this time Max was faster, landing a punishing jab on Clay's cheekbone, his hairy knuckles cracking hard against his temple. She swore she could hear bones crunching as Clay stumbled, the back of his head smacking hard against the brick wall of her apartment building. He grunted loudly from the pain, and all her instincts told her to run to him and comfort him.

"Stop! Please stop," she shouted, and she wasn't sure if she was talking to Clay or Max, or just praying to the universe for an end to this fistfight. But when she looked around, the street was empty, and she knew this was going to be between the two of them.

Clay lunged forward quickly, brushing off the double-blow like it was nothing, but Max went after him again, raising his fist and swinging hard. Clay dodged that blow, then Max threw another, landing one on Clay's shoulder that barely seemed to bother him. Especially since he grabbed Max's hand, twisted it around his back and yanked hard.

"Don't ever touch her again," he seethed, jerking the arm higher. Then he let go and reacquainted his fist once more with Max's jaw, sending the big man stumbling backward and landing flat on his ass on the sidewalk. Max was helpless, huffing in a heavy pile, staring up with wide-open eyes at the man who'd landed the final blow. With fists clenched at his sides and anger radiating off him in hot waves, Clay bent over him. "Now I'm giving you five seconds to get up and run the hell away."

Max nodded once, scurried to his feet, and took off down the street. When Clay turned to Julia, he was breathing hard and blood streaked from his temple down his cheek.

CHAPTER TEN

He flinched as she dabbed at the cut with a wet washcloth.

"It's okay," she said softly.

"I know," he muttered, rubbing the back of his head where he'd hit the building.

Kneeling between his legs, she gently cleaned the blood as he sat in her bathroom. "Does it hurt?"

"No."

She shot him a doubtful look. "Not even a little?"

"Not even a little," he said, but the expression on his face told her otherwise when she wiped off the last drop of blood. She reached for the Neosporin, applied some to the cut, and then opened a Band-Aid, pressing it gently along his temple.

"There," she said. "You look totally rugged now."

He managed a small laugh as she rose, dusting his other cheek with a kiss. Handing him two Advil and a glass of water, she said, "For your head."

He swallowed the pills and gave her the cup. She set it down on the sink. "Now let's get you out of your clothes and you can rest."

"I'm not resting," he said, rolling his eyes at her.

"You need your rest."

"It's only a cut. I've been cut worse at my gym," he said, and she knew he was trying hard to be the big, tough man. She was having none of that. He'd gone to the mats for her, and she was going to take care of him until he was no longer bloodied and bruised, and even then some.

"I don't care," she said, parking her hands on her hips and giving him a sharp stare. Then she bent forward and began unbuttoning his shirt.

"You're not taking off my shirt to go make me lie down in bed," he said roughly, trying to swat her hand away. She grabbed at his hands and stilled his moves.

"Oh yes I am," she said sternly. "Watch me."

She worked her way down his shirt, unbuttoning the fabric, spreading it open and gently taking it off, trailing her fingertips along his chest as she did. He moaned low and husky as she touched him. "Don't get any funny ideas, Mister."

"It wasn't a funny idea. More like a dirty one," he said with a sly grin.

She reached for his hand. "Come on. Bed. Now."

"Bed for other things," he said, but he let her lead him out of the bathroom and into her bedroom. She unbuttoned and unzipped his pants, then he stepped out of them. After laying the clothes neatly on a chair, she turned around to find him already in her bed, briefs on the floor.

"You're fast."

"Zero to undressed in no time," he said in a tired voice.

"We'll add that to your skill set."

"Come here," he whispered, resting on his side under the sheets. "Let me unzip your dress."

She moved to him, perching on the edge of the bed. He reached his hands up the back of her dress, those same hands that had defended her and protected her, and gently lowered the zipper on her dress, his knuckles softly grazing her spine as the dress fell to her waist. She shifted her body, so she could watch him. He smiled faintly as he unhooked her strapless bra. She stood and turned to face him, sensing he needed to show he could take care of her, even when he was the one hurting. She placed his hands on her hips, guiding them to slide the dress down her legs. Off came the shoes, then she curled up next to him in bed.

"Thank you," she said, gently tracing his other cheek with her finger. "For doing that."

"Julia," he said, pulling her in close. "I can't believe that's what you've been dealing with."

She sighed. "Yeah. That's my life."

"This needs to stop. You're not safe," he said, concern thick in his voice.

"He's not even usually the one assigned to me. My regular has the flu or something," she said, flashing back to Skunk's pale face and peaked look earlier that day.

"You can't keep doing this," he said firmly as the shadows from the moonlight streamed across the bed, casting the room in a blue midnight light. "So this is what I didn't get to say in the car. I play every week. With actors, clients, colleagues and some of my friends. It's not a rigged game. It's a real game with real stakes and real money. Come to New York this weekend, and join us. Play for real. Play in a game that's not a set-up where you're not hustling. And take us down. Win on your own terms," he said, and the idea took hold instantly, planting roots inside her. She craved that feeling—w*in on your own terms.*

His offer was so alluring, like a faint scent of some-thing delicious trailing through the air. But then, did she still know how to win on her own terms?

She scoffed out of self-preservation. "What if I lose?"

He scooped her hair off her neck, nuzzling her. "Where is my badass woman?"

"Huh?"

"*What if you lose*? I thought uou were a poker shark? Don't lose. Come to New York. Play your ass off. You're a card player. You don't come to lose. You play to win. So play, and win fair and square," he said, and there was something immensely appealing about his offer.

She quirked her lips in consideration. "It does sound like fun," she admitted.

"And if you lose—which you won't—let me pay him off," he said, his eyes locked on her the whole time. The look in them was intense, and true—he wanted this. He wanted to help her. She had always known he had this side, but now she was seeing it in action, and the gesture was slinking its way around her heart, loosening yet another layer of her stubborn woman-against-the-world attitude.

"Clay," she chided softly, lightly running her fingers along his strong chest. "I don't want you paying my debt."

"All the more reason for you to play hard."

She stared sharply at him, determination in her eyes. "I always play hard."

"I know you do."

"If I do this, you can't make it a rigged game. Don't make it fake."

"I would never do that."

"I want to win for real. Because I'm good."

"You're going to kick unholy ass. And if for any reason the game ends, and you're not in the black, I will take care of the debt. Deal?"

"I really don't want you paying it off," she said, grabbing his wrists for emphasis. "Promise me it's a real game, and we go to the end of the night. We play until everyone else folds."

"I promise you."

"I don't want to have to take your money. I want to prove that I can do this."

"And you will. I offer it as insurance. That's all. And that's why you'll win. Because you want to do this on your terms. Because the thought of anyone paying your way makes you dig your heels in like a batter at the plate swinging for the fences. Come to the plate. And hit it out of the park," he said, as if he were making a motivational speech.

A damn powerful one.

She wanted to say no, to insist on doing it her way. But he'd taken a hit for her. And he was offering her a way to fall in love with poker again and to win on her terms. He was offering to be there with her, for her, not to own her, but to help her. With every move he made, she was falling harder and harder, and she was sure there'd be no turning back from this man. She'd been so closed-off from the start about letting someone into her world. Now, he was all the way in, and the only thing she was afraid of was him not being part of her world.

So she did the thing she'd never have imagined doing a mere month ago. Hell, a week ago. "Then we have a deal."

"Good," he said with a happy, woozy smile as he lay flat on his back, pulling her on top of him, angling up his hips. He was growing hard against her. "Now I'm tired and I'm wounded and I could use a little — "

She cut him off. "There's only one true cure for a wounded man," she said, and went under the sheets. She stroked him to a full erection, then dropped her mouth onto him.

He groaned as she wrapped her lips tightly around his cock. He pushed back the sheets so he could watch her. She looked up at him, wanting him to see the desire in her eyes. His went dark and hazy as he stared at her mouth moving lovingly along his shaft. She tucked her knees up under her, getting into the perfect position for giving him the blow job he deserved.

She let him fall from her lips for a moment, but kept her hand wrapped around him. "Enjoy this. Enjoy everything I'm going to do to you, my gorgeous, sexy, wounded man who rescued me," she whispered, pushing her other palm on his flat abs, feeling his washboard belly as she returned her mouth to him. She took him in deep, the way he liked, and used her hands too, touching his stomach, squeezing a small, dark nipple, causing him to jerk his hips up hard into her mouth.

She moved her hands lower, down his body, stroking his muscular thighs, settling deeper into the space between his legs. He parted them, giving her room to get cozy, and she thrilled inside at how he gave his body to her, trusting her with his pleasure just as she had with him. She drew him into her warm mouth as far as he could go. She sucked hard and passionately, wanting him to feel flooded with sensations that blotted out any of the lingering pain from the fight. Cupping his balls in one hand, she slipped another hand under his ass, squeezing a cheek hard in her palm.

He groaned loudly in response, and the sound sent heat flowing through her body.

"I'll take another hit to my head for this," he murmured, his voice both weary and thoroughly needy. He reached for her head, threading his hands tightly in her hair.

She let go momentarily. "Pull my hair if you need to," she said.

He gripped hard as she returned to him, tugging her hair over to the side, yanking her head so he could stare hungrily at her face as she licked and sucked the full length of his fantastic cock.

"So fucking gorgeous," he said, outlining her lips with a finger, tracing the edge of her mouth as she held him tight and deep, swirling her tongue along his shaft the way he loved.

She was sure he groaned louder than he ever had as she worked him over with her hands and her mouth, touching him in all the ways that drove him crazy. His body was a playground for her fingers, and she ran them along his thighs, over his ass, and in that spot just under his balls that drove a man wild. He gave himself over to her, rocking his hips into her mouth as she traveled to his favorite places. A pinch there, a touch here, a squeeze of those sexy cheeks: she was showing him that she knew how to control all his pleasure too. Then, as she gripped his firm ass in her hands, she fucked his cock with her mouth until she felt the shudders roll through his body.

He grappled at her hair, his breathing turning wildly erratic as he gripped her head, thrusting and calling out her name as the taste of his release slid down her throat.

Minutes later, she nestled herself in next to him. With his arm wrapped around her, she kissed his neck, his stubbled jaw, his tender cheek. "You like it when I let you control me, and I like it when you lose control for me," she whispered.

"Mmmm," he murmured. "We are a good combo."

"The best," she said as she closed her eyes, feeling like they were partners in everything at last.

* * *

Another pair of Advil did wonders to mute the throbbing in his skull, but the dull ache was a useful reminder of what he was up against as he pushed open the door to Mr. Pong's shortly after noon the next day. The smell of fried pork and noodles filled his nostrils. Waiters bustled around delivering plates of pepper steak and lo mein to the lunch crowd.

It was your standard order Chinese restaurant with thick menus and illustrated pictures of the twelve signs of the Chinese New Year— such as horses, snakes and rats, along with an illustrated dragon image presiding over them all.

Fitting, he reasoned, as a hurried waiter rushed over to him.

"One for lunch?"

"No. I'm joining someone. You can tell Mr. Stravinski that I'm here."

The waiter looked confused. "Sorry. Who should I tell him is here?"

"Tell him the guy he's expecting to see."

"Okay," the waiter said, narrowing his eyebrows briefly at the request before turning on his heels to find the man in charge.

Moments later, a tall man in a sharp suit strode over to him. He had thick, dark hair and muddy-brown eyes and some of the worst teeth Clay had ever seen. He wasn't thin, he wasn't fat; he was simply the sturdy type.

He extended a hand to shake.

"Clay Nichols," he said.

"Charlie Stravinksi. I had a feeling I'd be seeing you. Come," he said, gesturing grandly to the restaurant as if he were quite proud of the joint he'd taken over on a debt that went belly-up. "There is a table for us near the kitchen."

"Fantastic," Clay said coolly, as if this were just another lunchtime business meeting.

After they sat, a waiter handed Clay a menu. "Thank you."

Charlie tapped the menu. "Everything here is delicious. But may I personally recommend the kung pao chicken," he said, bringing his fingertips to his mouth and kissing them as a chef does.

"Consider it done," Clay said, pushing the menu to the side. He had every intention of not only talking to Charlie, but breaking bread with the man. If there was one thing he'd learned in his years as a lawyer, it was that the more you knew about the opposing side, the better off you were. And the less fear you showed, the more likely you'd win the points you wanted. Besides, he had a hunch Charlie was the type of man who would act supremely gentlemanly to a worthy adversary.

Clay planned to be just that.

"So, you messed up the nose of my new guy," Charlie began, leaning back in his chair and crossing his arms.

"It got in the way of my fist."

Charlie scratched his neck, as if he were a dog itching fleas. "He shouldn't have been there. He's too hot-headed to be on the street."

"Yeah?"

Charlie shook his head, and blew out a long stream of air. A man frustrated, he placed his elbows on the table and steepled his fingers. "Stevie was supposed to give her the message, but he came down with the flu, he claimed," Charlie said with a scoff.

"I'm guessing that's the last time he'll duck out of work for a sick day," Clay said dryly.

Charlie laughed, throwing back his head and letting loose several deep chuckles. Then he took a deep breath, and the laughing silenced. "What are you here for?"

"Seems we have something in common, don't we?" Clay said, establishing first their mutual interests.

"Red."

"That's what you call Julia?"

"Yes."

"Here's the thing, Charlie," Clay began, keeping his voice completely even and controlled as he knew how to do. "Can I call you Charlie? Or do you prefer Mr. Stravinski?"

"Charlie is fine."

"So here's the thing," he repeated, leaning back in his chair, mirroring Charlie's moves. "You're going to need to go through me now."

Charlie arched an eyebrow. "I am?"

"You are."

"And why would I do that?"

"I'm her lawyer and I'm handling you. And that's how it's going to work. You want your money, I presume?"

"I would like it," Charlie said. "I am fond of money."

"I had a feeling you were, so I brought some extra

to settle some matters," Clay said, then dipped into his pocket for his wallet. Taking his time he opened it up, wet a finger, and counted some crisp bills. He laid $500 on the table. "This is for your guy. It's a way of saying I'm not sorry his nose ran into my fist, but I do aim to take responsibility for my actions."

Charlie eyed the money approvingly. "Go on."

He peeled off another five $100 bills, adding them to the stack. "This is for you to leave her alone this week."

A laugh fell from Charlie's lips. "It's going to cost more than that."

Clay added $500 to the pile, then raised an eyebrow in question. Charlie nodded. "That'll do."

"And this," he continued, adding five more to the pile, "Is a promise that we will have the $10,000 remaining on the debt to you by next weekend."

"Or?"

"There's no *or*," Clay said firmly, never wavering as his eyes remained locked on the man across from him. "It will be paid. And you will be done with her. Is that clear?"

"Why should it be clear?"

"Because that's how deals are done, Charlie. When the final $10,000 is paid, she's free and clear and I never want you to talk to her, be in touch with her, or send your men after her again," he said, his eyes locked on the man he despised, never wavering.

"Are you going to ask me to sign something? A legal contract, perhaps?" Charlie said in a mocking tone.

He shook his head. "They don't make contracts for this kind of deal. That's why I paid you the extra just now in good faith. Those are the terms of our contract. Good faith."

Charlie paused, and cocked his head to the side. Looked Clay up and down. Then his lips curled up. "I can live with those terms."

"And you can live with the other ones? When this is done, it's over and out?"

"If she has the money for me, I will not ever need to see her again," he said through gritted teeth.

"I told you. We will have the money. But she's not playing in your games anymore."

"Really?" Charlie said, doubt dripping from his mouth. "What is she going to do? Play the slot machines in Vegas to get my ten grand?"

Clay laughed and shook his head. "No. But does it matter? Do you care where your money comes from, or just that it arrives in a neat, green package?"

"Green is good. But I will be in New York next weekend. I'm moving a game there."

"What a coincidence. I happen to live in New York," he said.

"You will pay me there. By Sunday morning I want it. One week," he said, holding up his index finger in emphasis. "We will meet at eleven at my favorite restaurant in the Village. I will get you the name."

"Consider it done."

"And we will do business like men. We will shake on it when the deal is done."

"I'll be there."

The waiter arrived then with two orders of chicken and two sets of chopsticks.

"Dig in," Charlie said.

Clay took a bite and nodded in approval. "That's some damn fine kung pao chicken."

"As you can see, it would have broken my heart to drive this place to the ground like I could have. I kept it open for the chicken. It's rated best kung pao chicken in San Francisco. Nothing makes me prouder."

"It's the little things in life, isn't it?" Clay said, holding up a piece of chicken between his chopsticks as if in a toast to the dish.

"Indeed it is," Charlie said, a smile spreading across his face. "I like you. You have balls. You should work for me. I can always use a good lawyer."

"Thank you. But I'm going to have to pass on that. I have a pretty full client list at the moment."

They spent the rest of the hour talking about sports and eating chicken, and discussing whether San Francisco or New York had better restaurants. Though he didn't enjoy the time, and in fact, he spent the vast majority of it in a coiled state of restraint so he wouldn't strangle the man with his bare fists, at least he left understanding the enemy.

And that always counted for something.

CHAPTER ELEVEN

"How much do I bring to the game?"

Clay glanced up from the check, shooting Michele a quizzical look. "The game?"

"Yes," she said emphatically, holding her hands out wide. They'd just finished lunch at McCoy's on Madison, in between their respective offices. He tossed his credit card on the table.

"Saturday night. Your game," she added.

"You don't usually come to poker," he said as the waiter scurried by with plates for another table.

"Am I not invited?" She crossed her arms.

"Of course you're invited, Michele," he said, trying to settle her. He didn't want her to be irritated, but she seemed in a seesawing mood. "I was just surprised."

"Liam invited me," she said, drumming her fingernails against the table as if she were trying to get his attention. But he was paying attention already.

"Oh yeah? You guys are a thing now?" he said, though he knew the answer because Liam had called him a couple of weeks ago to make sure it was all right to ask Michele on a date. Clay had said yes in a heartbeat, and then had barely thought about it afterwards. He had a two-track mind these days—work and Julia.

"Sort of," she said with a shrug, as the waiter rushed over to the table.

"He's a good guy. He'll treat you right," Clay said, handing the waiter the check and the credit card. "Thank you," he said to the waiter.

"He is a good guy, so when he asked me to the game I said yes," Michele said, tapping the table once more. Then she took a deep breath, and spoke quickly, the words tumbling out. "And your lady friend is going to be there, right?"

"Yes, she'll be there. My lady *friend*," he said, sketching air quotes. "Her name's Julia."

Michele only knew that Julia was coming to the game. She didn't know about Julia's financial troubles. None of his friends did, because it was no one's business.

"Julia," Michele repeated, saying the name as if it had ten syllables and they all tasted bitter on her tongue. "So I can approve of her then," she said, changing her tone, seeming suddenly light.

"Sure," he said, going with it. Because, women? Who knew how to read them sometimes? And every now and then, Michele was impossible to figure out. "I'm sure you'll approve."

"I need to make sure the men I care about choose the right women for them. I worried about Davis. I worry about you," she said, reaching across the table to rest her hand on top of his.

Ah, he got it now. He understood what was going on with her. "You don't have to worry about me, Michele."

"But I do," she said, lowering her eyes.

"I know," he said, softly. She worried about a lot of things. It was her nature. She hated to see the people she loved get hurt. She'd been like that since her parents died, and Clay had wondered from time to time if she was trying to somehow prevent more hurt in the world. Odd for a shrink, but then he wasn't one to try to psychoanalyze anyone. "I know you worry. But I'm okay. You'll like Julia. I know you will."

"You think so?"

He nodded. "I do."

Something sad flashed in her eyes. "Do you ever think what would have happened if . . .?"

"If what?"

"If we'd . . ." she said, her voice trailing off as she gestured from him to her.

He raised an eyebrow. She couldn't possibly be referring to that kiss in college, could she? Nah. She must just be in one of those melancholy moods.

"If we'd have become something," she added.

"But we are something. We're friends," he said, reminding her of what she meant to him. "I can't imagine us not being friends."

"Right," she said, with a sharp nod as the waiter returned with Clay's credit card. "I can't either," she added, and she sounded resolute.

Or, as if she were trying to seem resolute.

After he said goodbye to her and walked up Madison, he mulled over her question. Why would she possibly want to know what could have been between them? The two of them being more than friends was the strangest notion to him. It was as if she'd suggested he start walking on his hands. It simply didn't make any sense.

But he had no more time to contemplate because when he returned to the office, Flynn was there with the Pinkertons to review the details of their next film. He rolled up his sleeves and settled in for the afternoon, his focus only on his clients, giving them his absolute best because in another few hours, Julia would be in his house.

* * *

As the plane began its descent, Julia flashed back on the last five days.They'd consisted of otters, poker prep, and packing for New York.

Kim had waltzed into work on Wednesday announcing she'd gone with otters for the baby's nursery, and minutes later she'd left early when she thought she was having contractions.

Turned out she'd just had heartburn, but Julia didn't mind shouldering the extra load at Cubic Z because the week had been blissfully uneventful. After Clay's talk with Charlie that past Sunday, Julia had operated in a sort of protective cocoon. No one, neither Charlie, nor Skunk, nor that asshole Max had bothered her, and they hadn't gone near Gayle or Kim either.

She'd played online poker in her free time, fiddling around too with some poker apps on her phone just to keep her skills sharp for Saturday's big game. She knew a few extra hours on a screen weren't going to make the difference. Luck would be a deciding factor, but she also had to be sharper than the rest of the players at Clay's game—the actor Liam Connor, who was about to open a new restaurant; the cable TV show producer Jay Klausman, whose show on drug dealers, *Powder*, was a huge hit; and Clay's friend, Cam. She'd researched Klausman and Connor and found bits and pieces of intel on their card-playing skills. The actor was a Leonardo diCaprio style player, someone who bet big and played for fun, but Jay, a shrewd producer, was the bigger threat. The wild card, though, was Cam. Julia had a hunch he'd be the one to beat. A man like that, used to taking chances, and possessing some kind of magical touch—he was going to be trouble for her.

This was the kind of trouble she thrived on though, and she was ready, reviewing her strategy once more as she walked through the terminal.

Clay had a last-minute meeting with a client, so she hailed a cab into Manhattan. He'd left keys for her with the guy who owned the coffee shop next door to his building, and she was secretly grateful that she wouldn't have to see him the second she arrived. She wanted to, oh how she wanted to, but sometimes, a woman wanted to be fresh and clean when she saw her man, and there was nothing quite like washing off a six-hour plane ride. When she reached his apartment, she opened the door, locked it behind her, and soaked in the silence and the oddly welcoming feel of his place. The last time she'd been here she bolted. Now, she felt like she belonged. He hadn't left a welcome basket on the dining room table, but the simple fact that he'd left the key said all she needed to know about him—*trust*. It was given, and it was shared, and there were no questions asked.

He trusted her. She trusted him.

She dropped her suitcase on the bedroom floor, and patted the side, touching the outline of the gift she'd picked out for him that was safely tucked inside. She shed her clothes and stepped under a hot shower.

As she wrapped a towel around herself ten minutes later, she didn't feel any pull to sift through his drawers or paw through the medicine cabinet. She wasn't a snooper, and there was nothing she needed to hunt out in his place. Besides, he was the definition of an open book, and there was something so reassuring about knowing that intrinsically. With Dillon, there were moments when he'd seemed a little shifty, from a joke here about not needing to report all the income he made from Charlie, to a little moment there when he'd told a story about stealing a milkshake glass from a diner in college. Fine, those were college hijinks, but as she looked back with 20/20 vision she could see hints of who he was.

Clay was the opposite—he didn't hide. He put himself out there for her from the start. No bullshit, and hell, she could use that in her life.

She hung up the towel, rubbed lotion on her legs, and went straight for his closet. Not to snoop, but to choose an outfit. She didn't need to rifle through her suitcase for jeans and a camisole when she knew what he wanted her in.

One of his shirts. She slipped one on, buttoned it to her breasts, and considered herself fully dressed.

She heard the door open, and her heart tripped over itself. Excitement tore through her body because he was here, and she damn near wanted to race down the two flights of stairs. But she knew this man, and knew what he wanted. He didn't need her running into his arms. He'd want to discover her. She padded down the steps quietly, turning the corner at the second floor just as he was leaving his phone and keys on the kitchen table.

She leaned against the top of the railing, her hip resting against the iron, her fingers toying with the top button. Waiting. Waiting for him.

When he looked up, his eyes locked on her face. He stroked his chin, and shook his head in appreciation.

"I could get used to this," he said, his deep, gravelly voice turning her to liquid as he stalked over to her, up the six steps, then cupped her cheeks in his big strong hands. "*You.* In my house. In my clothes. Here for me."

She melted as sparks raced over her skin. "All for you."

Neither one of them said another word as he looked at her as if he were inhaling her, as if the very sight of her was oxygen in his lungs. Electricity charged through her under his gaze. She wanted him to eat her up, to taste her, to touch her all over. Everywhere —this man needed to be everywhere on her body, in her body, in her heart, in her mind.

She reached for the collar on his shirt, gripping it hard. At some point they were going to kiss, they were going to crash into each other, but now the moment was heady with silence, drenched in anticipation of them coming together.

She stepped backwards, clutching his shirt. He followed, matching her until the back of her knees hit his couch.

Then it happened. Like fireworks, an explosion at the end of the Fourth of July, loud and powerful, that rang in your ears and lit up the sky. Everything became a frenzy of heat and vibrant color as he touched her. Before she knew it, the buttons on her shirt—*his* shirt—had scattered to the hardwood floor as he tore it off her. His shirt was gone next, pants unbuttoned, yanked down to his knees, then off. Like a leopard, he sprang fast, heated and fevered too, and before she knew it she was naked on her back on his couch, her legs up on his shoulders as he held her down hard with his big body. His arms, like steel, held her thighs in place as he entered her in one mind-blowing thrust. She was pinned, deliciously pinned, by this position. She couldn't move her legs, but her hands were free to touch his beautiful face, and she reveled in the chance to stroke his five o'clock shadow, to map his features with her fingers, to draw her thumbprint over his jaw that she loved.

Loved.

He moved in her, fucking her the way he kissed her, deep and consuming, in a claiming of her body. He was owning her, marking her, his fingers digging hard into her shoulders, clutching her tightly, as if he couldn't bear to let go. He took her hard and he took her slow at the same time. She felt him in her bones, on her skin, down to her very cells. He was inside her, he was outside her, he surrounded her. A symphony of sensations flooded every vein, and soon it became impossible to tell where one note ended and the next began. She could no longer distinguish between her body and her heart; they were one and the same, swallowed whole with longing for *him*. She and Clay had smashed into each other, atoms and particles colliding, combusting into this never-ending bliss.

"Do you think this will ever stop?" she whispered in between breaths.

"Wanting you like this?"

"Yes," she said, inhaling sharply as she held his face, never taking her eyes off his.

"No," he said, his voice ragged. "Because of how I feel."

"How do you feel?"

"I am obsessed," he said, raw and heated, his words touching down in her soul. "Utterly obsessed."

"The same," she whispered, barely able to form complete sentences, but not needing to. He took possession of her mouth, his lips devouring hers as he rocked deeper into her. He kept her restrained with his body, his arms, his cock, his lips, his tongue, his power, his control that he desperately needed to balance his obsession. She felt it all too, every ounce of him, of his desire and his need for her. Giving herself to him, she let him take her how he *had* to, because when he did, he brought them both over the edge.

She grasped his neck harder, holding on tight as pleasure ricocheted through her body, and the world spun so far into ecstasy that she never wanted to return.

Eventually she came back to earth, and he reached for her, nuzzling her neck, kissing her cheek, unable to keep his lips off of her. A kiss on her shoulder, another at the hollow of her throat. He stopped kissing her to trace her arm, holding her gaze as he did. "I want that every day. I want you every day," he said, his voice rumbling over her skin, drugging her with its sexy warmth.

"Me too. So much," she said, still high on him, them, the moments that had stitched together into bliss. Maybe that's why she felt bold enough to say the next thing. "It was different this time, Clay," she murmured.

"How?"

"I don't know. Maybe more connected. This is going to sound crazy, and you know I don't talk this way. But it felt deeper. Like we were the same," she said, a flush creeping over her cheeks as she opened her heart to him more and more every time. But she wanted him in now. She didn't want an arm's-length Clay anymore. "Does that make sense?"

"Yes. Do you know why it felt deeper?"

"Why?" she whispered, and the moment felt suspended, like they were on a bridge, holding hands, about to jump into the water below.

"Because there aren't secrets anymore between us," he said, brushing the backs of his fingers against her cheek, softly, oh so softly that she melted into his touch. "Because we're in this together."

"That's all I want. To be together with you," she said, the warm rush of falling blotting out everything else in the universe. Surely, nothing existed beyond these four walls. The city had disappeared and they were all that was left.

"No more lies. No more secrets. Only the truth," he said, his voice strong and steady.

"Only the truth," she repeated, and nothing had ever felt more true than this moment. "Like this. How I feel for you is like nothing I've ever had before."

"Me neither. I can't get close enough to you, Julia," he said, linking his fingers through hers, and that gesture, so tender and loving, was like stripping off a final layer. "I can't have enough of you. I want more of you. All the time."

"You can have all of me," she said, watching the reaction in his eyes. As if she'd given him all he ever needed with those words.

"You're all I want," he said, and it felt like a promise of what they might have together.

"What will you do with me after tomorrow night, once I have all this free time?" she asked, shifting from the intensity of their admissions to something a touch more playful, like they'd always been together. They'd had that from the start, from their very first night. She loved that they had so many sides.

"I figured you'd have your fill of poker, and be ready to move onto bridge. Strip bridge," he added, raising an eyebrow.

"We could try canasta, even. Or if you really want to go wild," she said, punctuating her words with a quick trip of her finger down his strong arm, "we could do Go Fish."

He pretended to fan out several cards in his hands. "Julia, do you happen to have any sevens?" he teased, as if they were playing the kids' game.

She mimed handing over a pair. "I'll miss my lucky sevens," she said with a pout.

"We'll make new luck. Because I know what we're going to do with all your free nights."

"What's that?"

"I'm going to take you to Vegas. Play for fun. We'll play blackjack."

"I'd love to go to Vegas with you."

"You can meet my brother. We'll go to Brent's comedy club, then I'm going to take you to one of those late-night clubs in the Bellagio, where it's dark and smoky and the music is low, and you'll dance with me."

"You dance?"

"Gorgeous, with you and me, dancing would be foreplay. I'd have you grinding against me on the dance floor," he said, flipping her around so her back aligned with his chest.

She wiggled her rear against him in demonstration. "Like that?"

"Yeah, keep practicing that," he said, low and husky in her ear.

"We'd play the slots, too," she added, keeping up their Vegas dreams.

"We'd lose money and not care," he said, brushing her hair off her shoulder. Planting a kiss on the back of her neck. Making her shiver.

"See a show."

"Fuck in a limo on the strip," he said, tracing her hipbone with his strong fingers.

"Fuck in the elevator," she said, sliding her leg through his, wanting to be wrapped up in him.

"Leave work behind. Leave the past behind."

"Not look at my phone. Not think about my phone."

"No one could reach us," he whispered. "We'd get drunk on each other."

She turned back around, needing to look at him, to see him. She ran a thumb over his lips, watching his eyes float closed as he hitched in his breath. "I'm already drunk on you, Clay."

"Stay that way," he said. "I need you to stay that way."

"I will."

CHAPTER TWELVE

He didn't want the time with her to end. He didn't want anything with her to end.

As he stepped into the elevator after dinner at an Italian restaurant that evening, he was painfully aware of the ticking clock marching towards tomorrow's game, then Sunday morning when they'd meet Charlie at eleven, then Sunday afternoon when he'd put her on a plane and let her crisscross the country. As they reached his floor, the thought of sending her home again was like a cut inside the mouth, an annoying reminder that couldn't be ignored. Because he wanted so much more with her. He wanted these moments to unfold every damn day.

But all he could do was make the most of this moment.

"I have a gift for you," he said when they were inside his home.

A smile teased at her gorgeous lips. "A gift? I love gifts. However did you know?"

"Of course you love gifts," he said, with the confidence of knowing her.

"Why do you say 'of course?'" She leaned against the doorframe in his kitchen, tilting her head to the side in curiosity.

"Because," he said, running his fingers across the top of her skirt. "Because you know how to enjoy things. Because you don't deny yourself. Because you let yourself feel pleasure and want. And that's the kind of person who likes gifts. The kind of person who knows how to enjoy life." He lowered his head to her neck, unable to resist brushing his lips against her soft skin. She shivered, and grabbed onto his shirt, tugging him close. "My point exactly," he added.

She broke the embrace and made grabby hands. "Gimme, gimme, gimme."

Stretching his arm around her, he scooped up the pink box that he'd left on the counter that morning. He handed her the gift, and tried his best to record every frame of her reaction. The way her eyes lit up as she ran a palm across the box, then as she untied the satiny white bow, letting it fall onto the counter. She lifted the top and peered inside.

"Ooh," she said appreciatively, then took the black thigh-high stockings from the box, and laid the box on the counter. "Your favorite thing."

He nodded.

"You want me to put these on now?"

"No. Save them. I need you to wear them tomorrow night."

She narrowed her eyes at him. "Why?"

"It's my poker handicap."

"What is that supposed to mean?"

"I don't want to win tomorrow. If you're wearing those, I won't, because it's all I'll think about," he said, brushing his fingertips from her knees up her thighs.

Her lips parted as he neared the apex of her legs, but she pressed a hand against his chest, holding him back. "I want to win fair and square. I told you that. You promised."

"I know you do. But you don't need to prove to me you can beat me, Julia. I'm on your team," he said, grabbing her hand and linking his fingers through hers. "And I need you to wear those tomorrow night for me. Say you will."

He watched her. Her shoulders rose and fell, and she didn't speak for a moment, as if she were considering it. "Why do you have to be so damn convincing?"

"It's my job to make a good argument."

"You're too good at what you do. But I'd wear them for you anyway. And since it's evidently Christmas early at your house, I suppose it's as good a time as any to let you know I have something for you."

"I love Christmas," he said as she took his hand and guided him upstairs. When she reached her suitcase, she unzipped it and dipped a hand into the inside pocket.

"This is a surprise, so close your eyes."

He did as she said. "I love surprises too. Did you know that?"

"No. But that suits you as much as you said my loving gifts suits me."

"Why do you say that?"

"Because of the time you surprised me at my apartment. And then at McKenna's wedding," she said, as her heels clicked across the floor, and he felt her near him.

"Hold out your hands," she told him, her sexy, sultry voice turning him on.

He opened his palms. "Put this on me," she said, and he felt soft fabric fall into his hands.

When he opened his eyes and looked down at his hands, he breath caught. A silk scarf was in his palms, and she was stripping off her clothes. "Blindfold me," she said.

He flashed back to their night in San Francisco last month. She'd told him it was the only thing she didn't want to do. "*The thought of it makes me feel a bit too vulnerable, and for a woman with trust issues, well, I'm not sure it's the best kind of kink for me.*"

"But you said," he began, but his words were swallowed dry as he watched her clothes fall in a heap on the floor, and she wore only her lace panties and heels.

"I know what I said." She ran her hand down his chest, her touch sending tremors through his body. "But things changed, and I want to do this for you. This isn't the same as you helping me out of my troubles, but even so, I want to give you what you want. Let me do this for you."

He shook his head. "Don't do this to say thank you."

"I'm not doing it to say thank you," she said firmly. "I'm doing it because I want to give you everything you want."

"You don't have to," he said, his voice hoarse, as he fought back the desire burning inside of him for *this*.

"I would never do something with you that I felt I *had* to. Everything I do with you I want to. I have so much want for you I don't know what to do with it all, but to give you more of it. So sit down," she said, and began to press her hand against him. She stopped. "Wait." Her lips curved into a wicked grin. "I don't think your fantasy is me telling you to sit down. You tell me what to do."

Oh, fuck. He was done for. His body was dangerously close to overheating, and she hadn't even touched herself. But this wasn't his fantasy for nothing. He knew how he wanted her—al fresco. "I want you on my balcony."

"As you wish," she said, her eyes catching his, a spark in them as she glanced back at him and headed down the steps, giving him a perfect view of her gorgeous ass as she walked. His cock twitched hard against his jeans as he pictured all the things he wanted to do to her ass. When she reached the sliding glass door and tugged it open, she cast her gaze to the outdoors, then crooked a finger, beckoning him.

"On the lounge chair," he told her, and she crawled across the cushions. He kept his eyes on her the entire time, savoring every move of her body as cars and cabs raced by five flights below. If he peered over the brick railing he could watch the Manhattan night roll along, the people walking down the cobblestoned street in the Village. But he wasn't looking anywhere except at her. She shifted to her back, her red hair fanning out over a pillow, her long, luxurious body stretched across the wooden lounge chair. A warm breeze floated through the dark night, blowing wisps of hair across her cheek.

He straddled her, running the end of the silk blindfold over her belly, her breasts, then her throat, so the fabric teased her skin. Gently, he pressed the material over her eyes. She lifted her head so he could tie it behind her. As he tightened the knot, she wriggled her hips against his pelvis, and he felt the heat from her against the fabric of his jeans. "You want this," he rasped out. "I can feel it. I can feel how fucking hot you are."

"I do want this," she whispered.

He lowered his head to her neck, buzzing a trail up to her ear. "I know you can't see anything now, but you can feel everything. That's why I want this. I want to watch you *feel* every single thing," he said huskily, licking the shell of her ear.

She looped her hands around his neck. "It's very dark where I am, and I need to know you're here the whole time. You can't look away from me."

"I promise I will have my eyes on you the entire time," he said, as he inched down her body. "You'll feel me."

"How?"

"Trust me, Julia," he said, as he settled in at the end of the lounge chair, giving him a perfect view of her body, a straight shot of her long, luscious legs. "I'm going to sit and watch you, and I'll tell you when I'm ready, and until then keep your hands at your sides."

She nodded, and he drank in the sight of her, from her beautiful breasts, so round and gorgeous, to her rosy nipples, hard and practically demanding to be sucked on, to her soft, flat belly. Then the thong panties between her legs, beckoning to him. His fingers ached to touch her there; his mouth craved her taste. She arched her hips ever so slightly as he stared at her legs, and it was as if she knew, without being able to see him, that he was looking at her with such longing and heat.

"You can feel me looking at you, can't you?"

She pressed her teeth into her bottom lip, and murmured, "Yes. I can feel your eyes on me."

"Good. Spread your legs," he said, and heat flared across his skin as she parted her legs, opening them wide for him.

He bit back a moan as he caught sight of the small scrap of fabric and the wetness on the cotton panel. This woman was so responsive, so aroused by him that it was almost a crime not to bury his face between her legs right now, send her hips shooting up into his mouth, and fuck her with his tongue.

"This is also how you'll feel me," he said, circling her ankles with each hand, then gripping them, and holding them down, her feet bound by him.

"Oh," she said, arching her hips and rocking into the cushion before she'd even touched herself.

"Now tell me how much you want to be touching yourself right now."

"I'm so turned on," she said, and her voice was hot and whispery.

"Are you aching to be touched right now, Julia?"

"Yes," she moaned, her mouth falling open as she licked her lips. "Can I?"

"Do it," he said. "Leave your panties on and slide those fingers between your legs."

She dropped her hand into the waistband, then lower, then lower still, and she drew a sharp breath when she made contact. God, it was a beautiful sight, her lips falling open as her fingers reached her pussy. He wanted those fingers to be his, he wanted his mouth on her, his cock inside her, but he wanted this torture more. He craved watching her, knowing how she looked when she was all alone. He wanted to witness how her body reacted to her own touch.

"Tell me how it feels," he said, as he gripped her ankles, her legs unbearably sexy in those heels.

"So good," she moaned. "So wet. My fingers are sliding all over, and I'm imagining it's your tongue."

Sharp agony rang in his body, and every instinct told him to tear off her panties and fuck her hard. But that wasn't the point. He needed the torment of seeing her naked body writhing in pleasure. He was hungry for the waiting, for the tension that gripped him as he forced himself to hold out until she'd already come from her own hand.

"And how does my tongue feel right now, Julia?" he asked as he stared greedily at her hand, moving quickly beneath the lace. "How does my tongue feel on your sweet little clit as I suck it between my lips and make you writhe into my mouth?"

She arched her hips into her hand, and moaned loudly, digging her heels firmly into the cushion. "Your tongue is so fucking good on me. I'm picturing riding your face right now," she said in a smoky voice that betrayed all her lust, all her want, and made him ache deep in his bones to touch her.

"Take off your panties. I need to see all of your pussy if you're getting this worked up so quickly," he told her.

She grabbed at the waistband, and pulled them down quickly to her knees. He tugged them off the rest of the way, taking them in one hand. "I need to smell you while you do this," he said, and brought her panties to his nose, inhaling her. The scent of her was a direct line to his cock, painfully hard beneath the denim of his jeans, begging to be freed.

"How do I smell?" she asked as she dipped her hand back down between her legs.

"So. Fucking. Aroused."

"I am," she said in broken breaths as she stroked faster.

"Let your legs fall wide open, Julia," he told her. "I want to see everything you do to yourself."

She spread her legs further, so beautiful, so vulnerable, so open on his balcony. A black scrap of silk over her eyes, heels on her feet, and her body that he desired every single damn hour of the day, here for him. He could take her now; he could yank down his jeans and thrust inside of her, sliding into the warm, wet home of her pussy. But he wasn't going to. Not yet.

"Are you touching yourself, Clay?" she asked as her fingers flew across herself.

"Do you want me to be? You can't see me."

"I know. But I can picture it. I want to know that your cock is fucking your fist right now," she said as she rocked her hips into her hand.

"You dirty girl with a dirty mouth," he said, with utter appreciation for the way she talked.

"I am, and you love it," she said, and the moment shifted from her submissiveness to her taking over somehow. He hadn't expected this, but then, she had a way of surprising him. "You love every filthy word from my mouth. You love watching me fuck myself, don't you?"

"God, I fucking love it so much," he said, hitching in a breath, and pleasure ripped through his bloodstream at the sights and sounds. "I can't think of anything that can get me off more than the woman I want fucking herself in front of me," he said, as he unbuttoned his jeans, slid down the zipper and let them fall to the ground. "I've been dying to know what you look like when you're getting yourself off to me. Now I'm going to find out," he said, rubbing his cock through his briefs. He wanted to close his eyes and give in to the pleasure, but there was no way he was missing this moment as her fingers raced across her swollen lips. "Show me. Show me now," he said, as he pushed down his boxer briefs and took his cock into his hand.

And there it was. A loud cry of pleasure. An exquisite moan as her back bowed and her hips shot up into her hand, her fingers flying fast and furiously. "This," she said, breathing hard, and erratic. "This is me picturing you licking me, eating me, fucking me, taking me. Any way you want. That's what I'm imagining now, Clay. Oh God, I want you so badly to fuck me now." She gasped, and her words were drowned out by her cries of pleasure as she rocked into her own hand, coming hard and beautifully for him.

In seconds, he was over her, untying the blindfold, watching her eyelids flutter open. Her pretty green eyes were hazy with lust. Never had he seen more heat in her gaze than in that moment. She'd loved every second as much as he had. He locked eyes with her as he reached for her hand, bringing it to his mouth and sucking on her index finger first, then her middle finger, licking her from her fingertips down to her knuckles so he could taste every drop of her.

"Perfect. You're so fucking perfect," he said, as he savored the taste of her desire in his mouth.

"Do you like?" she asked, all breathy, awash in the afterglow of her orgasm.

He shook his head, moving closer to her. "I *love*," he whispered, pressing the word softly against her lips. He kissed her eyelids, his way of telling her thank you for trusting him. Then he kissed her cheek, her neck, and her ear. "You're beautiful all the time, and so beautiful when you come with me."

"So was it everything you hoped it would be? Your fantasy?"

"Gorgeous, you are my fantasy come true," he said as he grasped her hand and wrapped it around his erection. Immediately, she stroked him, her soft fingers providing some kind of relief. He drew a deep breath, fueled by the electricity that shot through him from her touch. "I want to see those lips wrapped around me."

She let go, grabbed his hips, and pulled him down to her, lifting her mouth to him. The moment she made contact, he grabbed the top of the lounge chair. He had to hold back because all he wanted now was to fuck her mouth hard, and come in her throat. His bones were humming, his blood was rushing thick and hot, and he wanted the same release she'd had.

"No," he said, stopping her a few seconds later.

"Why?"

"Because I want it like this," he said and pulled her up to her knees, then pushed her down on all fours. "Because I need to touch you at the same time."

He guided his cock back to her lips, and she opened wide, taking him all the way in, her warmth surrounding him. He gripped the back of her head with his hand, her hair spilling over his fingers as he moved in her mouth. He slid his other hand along her back, enjoying the soft, smooth skin, then down to her ass, spreading his hand over one perfect check, and squeezing.

She caught her breath from that motion, even with her mouth full. He dropped his hand lower, slipping it between her legs. "Think you can handle being touched again right after you came?"

She nodded.

"Good. Because I was so jealous of your fingers the whole time I was watching you, and now I want my hand on your sweet pussy," he said, sliding his fingers over her lips, from her clit down through her wet folds, rubbing her in circles. She began to respond by rocking against his hand, moving her ass against him all while sucking him hard and as deep as he liked. Soon, he started to feel the build in the base of his spine, the threat of orgasm within his reach. All he had to do was thrust into her inviting mouth, let her take him as she wanted to. Every instinct in him said to keep fucking her mouth, especially given how she pushed back against his fingers, rocking into his touch. But that pussy, that delicious, beautiful pussy, was where he wanted to be right now. He gently reached for her, cupping her cheeks and pulled her off of him.

"You have no idea how much I want to come in your mouth," he whispered, holding her tight in his hands.

"So do it. I want to taste you. You know how much I love tasting you."

He shook his head, breathing hard, his chest rising and falling. "I want to look at you when I come. I want to watch your face when I make you come again. I want to be inside you."

She drew in a breath, and sighed sexily. "That sounds pretty damn nice too."

He sank down on the end of the chaise lounge, and shifted her on top of him. He reached for the blindfold behind him, and dangled it between her breasts. "I like my gift so much, and there's one more way I want to use it."

She somehow sensed his need before he told her, because she moved her arms behind her back, aligning her wrists along her spine. "Is this how you want me?"

"Yes," he growled. "This is one of the fifty million ways I want you."

"Are you going to tell me all the other 49,999,999 ways?" she asked playfully as he looped his arms around her.

He smiled as he tied her wrists together, and bound her forearms, until they were neatly restrained along her back. "How is it possible that you can do this to me?"

"I think you're doing things to me," she said, her lips curving in a grin.

He ran a finger along her lips, tapping her lightly. "No, funny woman. How is it that you can make me laugh as I tie you up?"

"One of my many talents with my mouth," she said, pouting sexily.

"Your sexy mouth is one of my favorite playgrounds," he said, grasping her hips, raising her up, and then lowering her gorgeous body onto his cock. She inhaled sharply as he filled her.

"The blindfold is the gift that keeps on giving," he said, and she smiled in return, then laughed deeply as he thrust into her, and he was sure it was her laughter that did him in. That melted his heart, absolutely and completely for this woman. He was there already, feeling everything for her, but for her to laugh like that during lovemaking, a joyous sound, sealed everything for him. He was a done deal when it came to her. She was the only woman he'd ever felt so much for, and he wanted her. Always.

* * *

She rode him up and down, but not a fast and furious kind of rhythm. More lingering and sensuous, taking her time, because they had time. There were no clocks, there were no deadlines; there was nothing but the two of them, entwined with each other.

He gripped her hips, guiding her moves at times, at others letting her set the pace. He kissed her breasts, burying his face against her chest, sucking one nipple, then the other. She desperately wanted to grab the back of his head and hold him tight against her, but her arms were shackled by the silk, and truth be told, she didn't mind one bit. She didn't mind being tied up by him, or tied down. Everything he did to her was designed to make her feel amazing—he fucked her like she was unbreakable, and he kissed her tenderly like her heart was the most fragile thing he'd ever touched, the thing he'd never want to break.

"I missed you this week," he said as he blazed a trail of kisses up her chest to her throat. "I missed you so much."

"I missed you too," she said, breathing hard as he filled her.

"I need to see you more, Julia," he said, and his voice was bare and emotional, stripped down to the simplest of needs.

"I need that too."

He looped his arms around her waist, then up her back, tilting his face to look at her as they made love. "Do you have any idea how much I want you?"

"Tell me," she said, locking eyes with him. "Tell me how much."

"I want you in every way possible."

"I thought it was fifty million ways," she said, teasing him, and he thrust hard in response. "Tell me some of them."

He gripped her wrists in one hand. "You know what I want? I want to fuck you in every way I can."

Her eyes widened with those words, with the possessiveness of his tone. "How?"

He dropped a palm to her ass, gripping her tight. "I want to fuck your pussy as I'm doing now." He drove deeper into her and she arched her back, letting him know she liked it. "I want to fuck your mouth, again and again," he said, running his finger across her lips, then sliding it into her mouth. She sucked long and hard. He dropped his hand to her chest, tracing a line between her breasts. "I want to fuck you between your breasts," he said. Then, in a flash, his hand had returned to her backside and he slipped a finger between the tops of her buttocks, causing her to draw a sharp breath. Inching his finger lower, she both tensed and thrilled as she sensed where he was going. He slid his hand between her legs, coating his fingers in her wetness, then began slowly traveling back up. "I want to fuck your hand, and I want to fuck your pretty little ass," he said, stopping to rub a finger against her rear.

"Oh God," she said, her eyes falling closed.

"Do you think you'd ever let me?" he asked, his voice all hot and husky against her throat as he pressed the tip of his finger further. He was barely inside her ass, but the twin sensations were so intense, tearing through her with a pulsing kind of tightness.

"I don't know," she admitted truthfully, in between breaths.

"Can I do this though?" he said, pushing deeper, and a bolt of pure, white heat lit up her body.

She could barely speak; words had become impossible to form. How could anyone put syllables together when he was inside her like *this*? When her entire body was trembling from pleasure, and from the unexpected intensity of both his cock and his finger penetrating her?

"Is that a yes?" he whispered, his voice low but firm. He needed an answer. He needed to know how far he could go, and there was a part of her that felt utterly helpless. She was tied up in his lap, with bound hands and spread legs. And yet, there was nothing he'd ever done to her that wasn't short of spectacular. He was a drug, and he delivered hits of pure pleasure through her heart, mind and body.

"Yes, you can do that," she said, swallowing thickly as he thrust his finger deeper. She'd never experienced this before, this double dose of intensity, but there it was, her entire body spiraling into a new land of ecstasy as he did what he'd said he wanted to do. He fucked her everywhere. He fucked her all over. He owned her and consumed her, and turned her world into blinding hot rapture as she rode him. He rolled his hips up into her, his cock driving deeper, his finger sending waves of pleasure through her. She was nearing the brink, racing to the precipice, and she needed to be closer to him.

"Untie me," she said desperately, through heavy pants.

Immediately, he undid the knot around her wrists, letting her hands fall free. She wrapped her arms around his shoulders, tugging him near, needing contact, needing to hold him as her orgasm vibrated wildly through her body. She gripped him tight, ecstasy carving its way through her in the most beautiful plundering, as he stole her body, her heart, and her very soul. She clutched him as his shoulders wracked with shudders too, joining her, his own grunts and moans piercing the night.

"I need you all the time too, Clay. All the time," she said into his neck, slick with sweat.

"I feel the same," he murmured stroking her back with his strong hands, and soon after she'd come down he carried her upstairs, turned on the hot shower, and bathed her, soaping her up and rinsing her off, then drying her, and taking her to bed, nestled and warm in his arms.

"We have to find a way to see each other more," he said, running his fingers through her hair as he faced her in bed, the dark of the night cloaking them, only a sliver of moonlight revealing his face. "It's not negotiable."

She arched an eyebrow. "Oh really, counselor? Is that how you play ball?"

"Certain terms are not up for negotiation. This is one of them."

"How do you propose you win this point in your client's favor? The client, I presume, is you?"

"You know what they say about representing yourself."

"That you have a fool for a client?"

He nodded, and smiled at her, his lips curving in that sexy grin. Then his expression changed. Shifted. Turned more serious. "Julia, when I first came to San Francisco, I had no idea *this* would happen."

"What's *this*?" she asked, nerves fluttering through her. She was terrified to attach definitions to what she was feeling. Better that he go first. He was always the braver one.

"You and me," he said, and the words made her heady. They'd both come so close to voicing the most dangerous one of all. "I didn't come to San Francisco that first night looking for this. I wasn't looking for anything."

"What did you come for? What did you want?"

"I didn't want anything," he said, staring deeply into her eyes. She felt as if he were looking far inside her, beyond her skin, beyond her cells, to know the heart of her. And that it belonged to him.

"And now?" She asked, her throat dry with hope.

His deep brown eyes searched hers, holding her gaze, holding her tight. "Now I want everything."

CHAPTER THIRTEEN

Her instincts had been one hundred percent right. Klausman, the show producer with the completely shaven dome and ever-present frown, had been tough as steel. He was hard to read and calculating, but she'd managed to separate him from about $1,000 by sticking to her guns, studying her cards, and quickly analyzing what had been played and what hadn't. Klausman was a fierce opponent; the guy showed no emotion, and he reminded her of how she played in Charlie's fake games.

Except tonight, she didn't play like that. She played loose and carefree on the outside, laughing and joking, and mixing a drink here or there at the restaurant Liam was slated to open in two weeks.

Speakeasy, he was calling it, and the place was gorgeous. There were booths in fine brown leather, and gorgeous oak tables, as well as a long, polished wooden bar. She loved that he hadn't gone with the overly slick look of so many bars and restaurants these days that draped themselves in chrome and steel. This restaurant was classy and warm, with rich red-framed abstract prints on the walls, and burgundy stools at the bar.

Liam finished dealing to Cam, then slapped down the last card for Klausman. He picked up his cards and considered them, his cold blue eyes on the hand in front of him. He'd never be the type invited into Charlie's games; he wasn't an easy target. Julia held her own cards, not too tight, not too loose, as Clay rested a hand absently on her thigh. His white button-down shirtsleeves were rolled up, showing off his fabulous forearms. He wore his purple tie, knotted loosely. His lucky tie, he'd called it. He puffed on a cigar, looking sexy and oh-so-masculine doing so.

But she wasn't focused on him right now. Her real focus was on Klausman, and she tried to study him, to gage his next move.

"Well, this is just a shit hand," Cam said out of nowhere, slapping his cards down with a loud smack, and shaking his head. "I'm so out I'm beyond out. They're going to need a new word for how out I am in this round." He brought the cigar he was smoking back to his mouth.

Julia smiled faintly at Clay's lawyer friend. He was exactly as Clay had described: big personality, big voice, lit up the room. He even smoked grandly, puck-

ering his lips around his cigar and taking deep in-
hales.

"So, Miss Julia," he said, "what is your favorite drink
to make? Absolute favorite in the entire universe of
spirits?"

"How about you let the woman play?" Clay said, as
Klausman pushed a black chip to the center of the table, muttering that he was in.

Cam's eyebrows rose at Clay's question. "What?
Your woman can't talk and play cards at the same
time?"

Julia raised her eyes. " Champagne for happiness.
Whiskey for loneliness. And vodka for anything else,"
she answered as she slid a chip into the pile.

Cam blew out a long stream of smoke, making rings
with his big mouth. "Well, look at that. She's a poet.
That was fucking beautiful. Was that not a beautiful
ode to drinking?" Cam glanced around the table, at
Liam, at Michele, at Klausman and at Clay, waiting for
them to respond to his question

"It was lyrical," Liam said, glancing up from his
cards to flash one of his charmer smiles. It was so
clear he was an actor, because he had that *it* factor,
the charisma that made him shine on stage. "Like a
gorgeous soliloquy." Tossing a chip into the mix, he
turned to Michele who stayed in the round yet again,
even though she hadn't once won. Julia had to give
her credit. The woman wasn't backing down, even
though she'd had nothing decent all night, and could

barely play. But she had iron nerves, and kept on ticking. Even Liam, who couldn't keep his hands off her, hadn't distracted her from her cards. Not when he nuzzled her neck, ran his fingers through her hair, or flirted like a movie star with her.

"I'm gonna drink to your ode to drinking," Cam said, holding up a glass in a toast across the table.

Julia raised an imaginary glass. "Cheers," she said, and soon it was time for hands to be revealed.

Clay went first, laying down his cards: only a ten high.

"Oh, you bluffing bastard!" Cam shouted. "Did you actually think you were going to win with that?"

He simply shrugged, and the corner of his lips quirked up. His secret? He was protecting her secret. "Man's gotta try," Clay said dryly, leaning back in his chair. He ran a finger over Julia's thigh as she placed her cards on the table, showing her pair of sevens.

"Lucky sevens," she said proudly, then she noticed Michele looking at her. Or rather, at her leg. At the exact spot where Clay's hand was, as he ran his finger across the fabric of her stocking. Maybe it was coincidence, or maybe there was something more to the stare.

Meanwhile, Klausman laid down his cards, and he had a pair of fives.

A phone rang, and Liam reached into his pocket. Glancing at the screen, he said, "My film agent. Let me go take this." He rose.

"Wait. Liam, what do you have?" Michele asked.

He waved off his hand. "I got jack shit. That's what I got. You show them my hand," he said, bending down to kiss Michele on the forehead. She tilted her face up and let out a small murmur. Maybe she did like him.

After he left, she shrugged and said, "I guess it's my turn. And I think I might have won my first hand," she said, showing two kings.

Julia's chest tightened and annoyance threaded its way through her body. *Damn.* The last person she'd expected to win was Michele. But then she told herself to let go of the annoyance. This was poker, and you didn't win every hand. Besides, she was having fun *not* playing with Skunk watching over her. Not having to show her cleavage to take down a VC. She had her eye on the prize, and she planned to snag the brass ring of victory, and then march into the breakfast meeting with Charlie tomorrow, shove the greenbacks in his face, and tell him to kiss the fuck off.

Klausman pushed back from the table. "Since there's a break in the action, I'll take a break."

Julia turned to Cam, who was finishing his scotch. "Want another?"

"I would love one," he said.

Michele waggled her empty glass. "I could use another. I'll join you."

"Sure. We'll make it a ladies night behind the bar."

* * *

She was beautiful. She could hold her liquor. And she'd known him for years.

"Here's your scotch," Julia said, sliding the glass to Michele, who brought it to her lips and took a swallow.

Julia knew she shouldn't be jealous, not after what she and Clay had shared, but this woman was *here*. In New York City. She could see her man anytime she wanted to. Julia studied her as she drank, that pretty brown hair, those gorgeous brown eyes, and her body. But she fought back the sliver of envy that snaked through her. She'd never been the jealous type. Had never been the insecure type either, and she certainly wasn't going to start down that road tonight. Women didn't need to battle each other or be bitchy.

"You two seem pretty happy," Michele offered once they were out of earshot of the men.

"I suppose you could say that," Julia said with a grin. "And what about you and Liam? He's rather fond of you."

"Oh. He's great," Michele said quickly. Too quickly.

"When did you start seeing him?"

"A few weeks ago."

"He's very sweet. And quite a charmer."

"You and Clay haven't been together for very long either, have you?" Michele asked. She clearly had no interest in discussing Liam.

"Two months."

"That's really not much, is it?"

"I don't know. Is it? Isn't it? Sometimes I think it takes all the time in the world, and sometimes it takes no time," she said.

"You're crazy about him, aren't you?" Michele said, and her voice sounded sad.

Julia rested her elbows on the bar. "I am. Absolutely. In every way."

"I can tell," she said, casting her eyes down at her glass.

"I'm glad it's obvious. Are you okay, though? You look . . ." Her voice trailed off as her bartender instincts to listen to patrons' woes kicked in.

Michele raised her eyes, and fixed them on Julia. "I want him to be happy," she said firmly. "My brother and I care deeply for him. We've been friends ever since college." Then she added, "Clay and I."

"He mentioned you went to school together."

"He was there for me when I was having a hard time with my parents' death."

"I'm so sorry to hear that."

"It was a while ago. But I had a hard time with it in college, and he was there for me," she said, and it was the second time she'd voiced that word – *college*. She glanced over at Clay as he chatted with Cam, blowing streams of smoke. Clay reached for his phone, flicking his thumb across the screen casually. *Strange for him to be on his phone,* Julia thought; he rarely was. But then he put it away quickly.

"I'm glad he was there for you," she said, and Michele simply nodded, barely listening as she looked at Clay. That's when it hit her—it hadn't been a mere coincidence when Michele had watched his hand on her thigh earlier in the game. It wasn't a coincidence at all. It was a sign of longing, and now Julia knew something about Michele that Clay didn't know. Something that Michele had been hiding for years.

Or maybe he did know that she longed for him. Maybe he simply hadn't told Julia yet.

That possibility pissed her off, but somehow she'd have to use it to fuel the game.

CHAPTER FOURTEEN

Two hours later, she'd pushed thoughts of Michele aside. Clay was with her and only her. Julia might be possessive, but she was not a jealous woman. How could she be jealous when she was closer to her goal? She was almost halfway to the prize, and Liam was making bigger and bigger bets. God bless an actor like him. He was simply flush with cash and didn't seem to mind parting ways with it.

She revealed her two aces, and Liam laughed, shaking his head. "Got me again," he said, shoving all the chips to Julia since everyone else was out for this hand.

Another step closer. She felt buoyant, bubbles rising to the surface. She could do this. She could win on her terms. Be free of her debt. The way she wanted to, by clawing her way out of her troubles. The prospect of not having to rely on Clay's bailout sent a surge of adrenaline through her. She didn't want a safety net.

Her blood pumped faster, turbocharged with anticipation. She could taste freedom on her tongue, like sweet sugary crystals, and that drove her as they played another round, then another, and each time, she added to her totals.

Clay leaned in to nuzzle her neck. "You're winning, gorgeous. I knew you would."

"Don't jinx me," she said softly.

"No jinxes. Just complete confidence in you."

A blast of pride raced through her. He was proud of her because she was good, because she'd earned it. Clay was the opposite of her ex. Dillon had taken her for a ride and fooled her. Clay was upfront about everything, and he believed in her. He'd never try to hoodwink her. "I'm glad you feel that way about me," she said as he knocked back a scotch. "Want me to freshen that up for you?"

"No, bring me a Purple Snow Globe or a Heist. The drink you named for me. Or wait. I have a better idea. Make me a new drink and call it the Long Distance Lover," he said, wiggling his eyebrows.

She laughed. "You want me to whip up an impromptu cocktail? You don't even like mixed drinks."

"I might if you made me one, but I'd probably just want to lick it off of you," he said, his dark eyes raking over her.

"You're drunk."

"I assure you, I would lick it off you sober, drunk, bone-tired, or sick as a dog," he whispered in her ear, flicking the tip of his tongue over her earlobe.

"I'm changing your name to Captain PDA."

"What can I say? I have my woman here with me, and I'm out with my good friends. All is well in the world," he said, then pulled back to catch Liam's attention across the table.

"Liam, we have a bartender in the house. Let her show you how much you wish you had her drinks on your menu here at Speakeasy."

Julia rolled her eyes, and pushed his shoulder. He grabbed her and kissed her on the lips.

"Man, do I need to book you a room at the Plaza?" Cam said, slamming his hand on the table.

"Yeah, 'cause we know you have connections everywhere," Clay said.

"Hey, I told you I got out of that racket."

"Well, you two boys just keep up the chest thumping, and I'll go a-mixing," Julia said, heading to the bar. She perused the offerings, considering gin, vodka and rum, then decided to start with a tequila as the base, adding in some fruity mixers, a little lemon soda and then something special—a secret ingredient. She held up a glass when she was done. "Who wants to be my guinea pig for the Long Distance Lover?"

Liam raised a hand, waving broadly. "My place. I go first." He trotted over to the bar, brought the glass to his lips, and tasted. "Mmm, this is superb," he said, smacking his lips. "You're like a mad scientist of the liquorian variety."

"Call me a chemist. I'm all about new flavors," she said with a big smile.

"You need to text me the recipe."

She shook her head. "A good bartender doesn't give up her recipes for free."

"Then give me your number and we'll make a deal for it."

She pointed her finger at him playfully. "Now you're talking," she said, and rattled off her number.

Liam spun around and used his big stage voice to call out to the table. "Everyone needs one of these."

After whipping up more cocktails, she returned to the table and served drinks to the rest of the players.

"Mmm, I love it," Clay said to her after he tasted the drink. He was pretty carefree and happy. Maybe it was the alcohol loosening him up. Or maybe it was because she was winning. He pulled her into his lap.

"Since when do you like mixed drinks?"

Julia looked up to see Michele asking Clay the pointed question.

"Every now and then I like to break out of my habits," he said.

"You're always a scotch drinker," the brunette added pointedly, and there was something protective in Michele's voice. Almost like a lover, or an ex. An ex who knew things about someone. "You were never like that in college."

"I was never a lot of things in college."

College. Julia's ears pricked at that word. Why on earth did Michele keep hearkening back to college with Clay?

"You were some things," Michele said.

"C'mon, enough about drinks and college. Time to deal," Klausman said gruffly, and started doling out the cards.

Julia slid off Clay's lap and back to her own chair. *Focus,* she told herself. She was almost there. She had to keep riding this wave of luck and skill to the tune of another few thousand dollars and she'd be free and clear.

She appraised her cards, and soon the betting began. Then the strangest thing happened. Michele won the next hand. And the next. And the next. With each successive win, Julia grew more tense, and she noticed Clay's light-and-easy mood slip away. He was no longer leaning casually in his chair. He was more focused on the game, his eyes shifting back and forth, and he kept looking at his watch too. The ticking clock, winding down to Charlie.

Michele cleaned up once more with a full house that made Clay sit up straight in his chair and reach into his back pocket. Maybe for his phone. But then he stopped, resting his hands on the table, and checking out Julia's dwindling stack of chips.

By the time the woman who'd known him since college had sliced Julia's winnings in half, she was ready to lunge at her and it had nothing to do with her staring at Clay, but everything to do with how jealous Julia was of Michele's hands all over the money she needed.

She probably didn't even need it. She'd probably use it for a goddamn spa weekend, not to pay off a mob boss.

"I swear it's beginner's luck," Michele said with the kind of laugh that sparkled. A pure laugh, a happy laugh, but it grated on her to no end because Julia wanted those chips to herself. "I have no clue how to play."

"What are you going to use your money for, baby?" Liam said, leaning over to kiss her on the cheek. "Take me out someplace nice, will ya? I want to go to the Bahamas again."

"Yes, and have your picture taken by someone trying to sell you real estate."

Julia latched onto one word—*Bahamas*. And it nagged at her brain. "My ex is probably in the Bahamas," she muttered.

Clay's eyes snapped up. "Dillon?"

She shrugged. "He always said he wanted to go there," she said in a low voice.

"He did?" Clay whispered.

"Yeah, but everyone wants to go there. He could be anywhere," she said, and something inside of Julia coiled tightly, like a viper rising through her chest. Maybe it was her mention of Dillon. Maybe it was

AFTER THIS NIGHT · 183

Michele's carefree way with money. Or maybe it was the simple fact that when Liam kissed Michele's neck, her eyes didn't flutter closed. She didn't part her lips to sigh. And she didn't slide her body closer to his.

Instead, Michele peered out of the corner of her eye at Clay. And the look in her brown eyes was one of such deep longing, and something more. Something much more. In a blinding moment of clarity, Julia no longer sensed that Clay hadn't been truthful about their relationship. She *knew*. There was something more to them, and she didn't care about the game, or the money, or Charlie. She cared about whether she'd been played again.

She pushed back from the table. "Excuse me," she said, and she tapped his shoulder and cleared her throat. "I need to step outside for a second, and get some fresh air."

"I'll join you," he said, rising and resting his hand on her lower back as she walked to the door, pushed hard on it, and then felt the rush of warm night air on her face. It was close to midnight, and the city was still lively, cars and cabs and people racing by.

"What happened in college between you and Michele?" She crossed her arms.

"What?" he said, blinking his eyes.

"Were you involved with her?"

"No."

"Did anything happen with her?" she asked once more, and this time she felt like the lawyer, turning over the question again and again until the witness answered.

"What do you mean?"

"Do I need to spell it out?"

"Yeah. You do," he said firmly.

She pretended to mime sign language as she spoke. "Were you involved with her? Because I'm getting a serious vibe from her that she's tripping down memory lane from the days of old," she said, now holding her hands out wide. "*College this. College that.* Clay in college. It's like she's holding on to something in college with you."

"We kissed once. We weren't involved."

He said it so matter-of-factly, but it slammed into her, and she nearly stumbled backwards. He reached for her, but she held him off. She was fine. She didn't need him.

"Ohhhhh," she said, long and exaggerated. "Right. Of course. A kiss. That's not involved what-so-fuck-ing-ever."

"What the hell, Julia? I was never involved with her. She's a friend. Not an ex-girlfriend."

"You kissed her," she said, jutting her chin out at him. "That makes her kind of an ex, wouldn't you say?"

"I don't think that constitutes an ex." The low-key way he answered her pissed her off, because he truly seemed to believe his own line of bullshit.

"Okay, let's get technical and legal about it then, if you're going to be like that. So I'll walk you through what constitutes being involved. When you've kissed someone, and I ask 'Were you involved with her?' that's the moment when you say 'Yes, I kissed her once, Julia, and it meant nothing to me, and we've been great friends ever since then, and I have drinks with her every Thursday night and talk about you, but don't worry that I had my tongue down her throat because we're just friends.' It's not at the fucking poker game I'm losing that you tell me," she said, practically spitting out the words through her anger.

"Are you pissed because you're losing, or are you pissed that I kissed her?" he asked her through narrowed eyes.

Anger flared deep inside her. Anger over that woman. Over Charlie. Over the three thousand miles between her and Clay. Anger, annoyance and frustration all fused into a cocktail of heat and rage as she grabbed his shirt collar. "Thanks for pointing that out, because it's kind of both. I have a shitstorm of trouble waiting for me back home if I don't win," she said.

"That's not true. I told you I'd help you," he said, and his hand moved briefly towards his pocket, but then he stopped.

"Why do you keep reaching for your phone? That's not your style."

"Flynn is out with the Pinkertons. Just wanted to make sure it's all going well," he said, then shifted quickly back to the matter at hand. "But I wish you'd stop worrying about the game. You're going to be fine."

"I don't want you to help me, though. I want to win on my own," she said, and she was damn near close to digging her heels into the sidewalk. Didn't he *get* it? Didn't he understand how important this was to her? But everything had collided right now. The game; Michele; the possibility of truth and lies.

"And you will."

She pushed her hands through her hair. "I just wish you'd told me when I asked you in San Francisco if you'd been involved with her. I asked you if Michele was your ex and you said she was just a friend, and always had been. But now it turns out you kissed her," Julia said, but she knew deep down it wasn't the kiss that bothered her. That wasn't why she was upset about Michele.

"It just wasn't important, but it's not as if you've been totally honest with me."

"I didn't lie, though. I told you there were things I couldn't tell you."

"I feel like we're parsing words here. I don't understand why it matters that I kissed her. Hope this doesn't come as a shock to you, but I've kissed other women before."

"I know," she hissed.

"So why does it matter so much that I kissed Michele once? I don't even think about her like that."

"Because. Because she is here, all the time. Because she sees you. Because I don't get to."

"We can change that," he said, his voice suddenly soft, all the harshness banished from his tone.

"How? I live far away and she lives a block away," she said, dropping her face in her hands, hating the sound of her own voice. "Ugh. Look what you've done to me. I've become this whiny woman pining away, and she's lovely and smart and funny, and it pisses me off that she can see you any time she wants."

He gently peeled her hands away from her face, tucking his finger under her chin and lifting her gaze to his. "I don't feel a thing for her. I didn't tell you when you asked if she was an ex because I don't even think about her like that. I don't think of her as an ex. It was one kiss, one time, one drunken night. Nothing more. I don't think about her because you're all I think about. To the point that I'm sure no man has ever felt this way for a woman. You shouldn't be jealous of her. She should be jealous of you."

She stared at him, narrowing her eyes. "Seriously, Clay? Cocky much?"

"It has nothing to do with me, and everything to do with how I feel for you," he said, moving his hands down to her arms, holding her tight. "Every woman should be jealous of *you* because of how I feel for you. Because no man has ever wanted a woman like I want you. No man has ever craved a woman as deeply as I crave you. And no man has ever fallen this hard and this fast for a woman."

Her heart stopped, then thundered furiously against her chest, wanting to leap into his hands. "I'm sorry," she murmured, all her anger draining away. "I'm a jealous witch. It's just hard for me to see her and know you're so friendly, and that she's so in love with you."

He froze like a statue. Then seconds later, though it felt like a minute, he looked at her as if she'd just spoken Russian. "What are you talking about?"

"You don't know that?" she asked, shocked.

"No."

"It's patently obvious to anyone who spends ten minutes with her. She's madly in love with you, Clay."

He swallowed, and shook his head, as if he were shaking the strange notion away. "How can you tell?" he asked, the words coming out all choppy.

"Because of how she looks at you," she said, as if it were obvious, because to her it was.

"And that's enough for you to conclude she's in love with me?" For the first time ever she'd truly surprised him. She hadn't intended to drop a bomb, but he so clearly didn't see it at all.

"Yes."

"Why? How? How can you tell she looks at me like she's in love with me?"

She rolled her eyes. "Because I recognize the look."

The look on his face was no longer shock. It was hope, and the dawn of something so much more. "You do?"

Then she realized she'd practically said it. "Yes."

"How?"

"Because it's how I look at you," she said, the words falling from her lips in a tumble. Time slowed, and the moment became heady, rich with possibility. The air between them was charged, electric, like a storm. They were magnets, needing their opposite.

He reached for her, cupping her cheeks, brushing his thumb over her jaw then her bottom lip, watching her shiver. She looked up at him, and his eyes were fixed on her. Waiting for her. His lips parted, and she was wound tight with anticipation of what he'd say. "I love the way you look at me."

Tingles ran down her spine, spreading to her arms, her fingers, all the way to her toes. "You do?

"I do. I love the way you touch me," he said, taking her hand, and spreading her palm open on his chest. "I love the way you talk to me. I love everything about you. And I recognize the look in your eyes, too. Do you know why?"

She shook her head, and her entire body was trembling with want, with hope. "Why?"

"Because it's the same as in mine. Because I love you, Julia. I am completely in love with you, and I love you, and I want you to love me," he said, never breaking his gaze from hers, his beautiful brown eyes flooded with love.

"I do. I do. I do," she said quickly, the tension in her chest disappearing, and relief washing over her in waves. "Clay, I love you so much."

He ran his hands through her hair, burying his fingers deep. She felt him trembling. He returned a hand to her face, brushed the backs of his fingers against her cheek, and she leaned into him, savoring the gentleness of his touch. Feeling the reverence that he treated her with, like she was precious to him. He ran his hand down her neck to her throat. "*Julia*," he said, his voice low but so intense as he spoke. "I have never fallen in love like this."

His words bathed her in some kind of bliss, as if her veins flowed with liquid gold. "How have you fallen?" she asked, overwhelmed with all she felt for him, with the way her body seemed to reach for him, to need him.

"With everything I have. There is no part of me that isn't in love with you. There is no part of me that holds back," he said, his voice steady, certain.

Allness. That's what it was for her, too. An utter *allness.* A love so deep and consuming it filled her organs, it rode roughshod over her skin. It was a mark on the timeline of her life. Before. After. She raised her hand, and touched his face, stroking his jawline, watching with wonder as she made him gasp after a simple touch. He grasped her hand, linked his fingers through hers, and brought her palm to his mouth, kissing her there. "I love you." He bent his head to her neck, brushing his lips ever so softly against her skin, then up to her ear. "I am so in love with you," he said, as if he couldn't stop telling her. "I love you so much."

"I am so in love with *you*." She stretched her neck so he could kiss her freely as he wanted to as she ran her hand through his hair. "So in love."

He stopped kissing her, pulling back to look her in the eyes once more. His gaze melted her from the inside out. "I can't wait to take you home with me tonight. To spread you out on the bed. To make love to you all night long."

"I want that. I want that again and again. And over and over."

"Now go back in there," he said, gesturing to the restaurant. "Even though you look like you've just had sex."

Her cheeks felt rosy. She was sure there was a glow in her eyes. "I feel like I've just had sex. Sex with the man I love," she said, playing with his hair, not wanting to let go of him, but needing to.

"You will have that. I will give you everything, Julia."

* * *

He'd join her shortly. He would. He just needed to take care of this matter. The text on his phone was loud and clear. Business came first right now, and later, he'd find a way to explain.

CHAPTER FIFTEEN

Julia skipped down the sidewalk at two in the morning. Every move she made brought a smile to his face, and touched down with happiness in his heart.

She'd done it. She'd won big. After precariously losing to Michele for a while there, she'd made a few big bets on a few big hands, and had pulled out ahead. She'd wrapped her arms around the chips, and tugged them in tight. She sure looked like she wanted to kiss them, to bring each and every one to her lips, and then shake them at the sky victoriously. Instead, she'd stacked them, handed them to Liam since he'd acted as the bank, and watched with wide eyes as those chips turned into cash.

She threw her head back, twirling on the street, as if she were a kid catching snowflakes on her tongue.

"And here's your money, sir," she sang, pretending to hand it over to Charlie. "Now, go fuck off forever."

She was jubilant, ready to lead a victory march. Clay grabbed her arm and pulled her in for a kiss, bending her back and kissing her like they were on a postcard. Let the whole damn city be jealous. Let the world want what he had. He claimed her mouth with his own, kissing her hard and passionately, like he planned to always. He'd never tire of the way her lips tasted, of her sweetness, of how she responded to him. She wrapped her arms around his neck, and held on tight.

"Take me home, now," she said. "I want to know what it feels like to have you as a free woman."

He tensed briefly as she said that. But that was ridiculous. She *was* free. Completely free. He hailed a cab, and ten minutes later he had her in his home, stripping her clothes off as they somehow made their way up the stairs, tangled up in each other. He was still buzzed on the night, on the things he'd said, on the way she'd won, on her sheer and utter happiness, and on telling her he loved her.

It didn't matter that one of those things was a lie.

There would be time in the morning to tell the truth. When day broke, and the sun rose, that's when he'd let her know. The night was for *more.*

"Did I ever tell you I have a thing for mirrors?" he said as he left his clothes in a heap on the floor.

She raised an eyebrow, as she stepped out of her skirt. "Then join me in the bathroom, handsome," she said, taking his hand and guiding him to the spacious room. She hopped up on the sink with the mirror behind them, roped her arms around his neck, and pulled him in close. Resting her forehead against his, she ran her hands down his naked chest, making him shiver with desire. "Thank you, Clay," she whispered. "Thank you for doing that for me. I can't tell you how much it means to be free of Charlie, and free of Dillon on my own terms. And I loved it. I loved playing for real. Playing in a game that wasn't fake. Where I had to rely on chance and skill and myself," she said, and her words were like a tight knot in his gut. But he let her continue. "It means so much to me. *You* mean so much to me. I am so glad you walked into my bar, and into my life, and into my heart."

He kissed her softly, brushing his lips against hers. At least this part was true. This contact. This touch. "That's the only place I want to be. In your heart," he said, then took a beat. "Though I like being in your pants, too."

She laughed. "Then get in my pants. Except I'm not wearing any," she said, gesturing to her naked body, covered only in the stockings he'd bought for her. "So this ought to be really easy."

He shoved everything else aside, clearing his mind. He wanted to be with her completely. "Nothing worth having is easy," he said, lifting her off the counter and setting her down on the tiled floor. He shifted her around so she faced the mirror above the vanity, then spoke low in her ear. "I want to watch us. I want you to watch us."

She gasped a yes as he dipped a hand between her legs, running his other hand up her belly. He entered her slowly, rolling his hips, savoring the delicious wetness, the tightness. Her eyes floated closed as he rocked into her. "Look in the mirror," he told her, and she opened her eyes, meeting his dark eyes in the reflection. There was so much want in her gaze, so much openness. "*Watch*."

"I am," she said, breathing in, breathing out. "I am watching."

"What do we look like to you?"

Her eyes were hazy, her lips falling open.

"Like two people in love," she answered.

He nodded against her neck. "Exactly. That's what we are. And I'm going to take you there, Julia. I'm going to take you over the edge. Because I love fucking you, and I fucking love you," he said, tugging her tighter, holding her closer as he thrust into her. She stretched out her neck, leaning against his shoulder, her body becoming a canvas for his hands as he touched her breasts, her belly, her neck, and her throat. He wrapped one hand around her throat, not so tight that it hurt, but tight enough to let her know she was his. He was possessing her. "Tell me you're close."

"So close."

"Tell me who's fucking you right now."

"The man I love," she said in between broken breaths, her lips open, her green eyes watching him in the mirror.

"That's right. The man you love is fucking you. The man you love is making you come," he said, watching her face contort in pleasure, feeling her body tighten on him, feeling her heat all over him as the sound of her ecstasy rang in his ears and he followed her there, chasing her to the other side.

He breathed out hard, and so did she as he wrapped his arms around her when they were done.

"Julia," he started, and he should have been nervous or scared, but he wasn't. Not one bit. He knew what he wanted. "I hate the thought of you going home tomorrow afternoon."

"Me too, but I have to."

"I know, but what if you come back, and this bathroom becomes our bathroom? And the bedroom becomes our bedroom? And this home becomes our home? I can't stand being without you. I want you here in New York."

He searched her features, but her expression gave nothing away. Her mouth was set in a line; her eyes were stoic. He tried to read her, to understand what was going through her mind, but he came up empty. And that's when the real fear shot off inside him. Had he scared her away? Asked for too much from a woman who needed to live life on her terms? He opened his mouth to backpedal, to say he'd take what he could get, because a little of her was better than losing her.

But then she turned around, face to face. "I could give you some long answer about how that's too hard or too complicated, and how I don't know how to pull it off or make it work, and how I have a job and a family and a business in San Francisco, and that's all true . . ." she said, then stopped talking, and in that silence his heart thumped hard against his chest, and he swore she could hear every heartbeat of his fear, could tell that each persistent pound was the soundtrack of his misery, of her leaving him.

"And?" he asked, his throat dry.

"And," she answered, the corner of her lips curving up, "and if you're willing to work with me and help me figure all that out, then I can't give you a single reason why this shouldn't be my bathroom, because I love your tub," she said pointing at the tub, and a smile broke across his face. She leaned back and tapped the mirror. "And I love this mirror." She gestured to the bedroom. "And your bed."

"Our bed," he said, correcting her.

"*Our bed.* I love our bed. Now, take me to bed, handsome. Because I want to sleep in my home. Tomorrow we can figure out all the details."

Yes, tomorrow. There were so many details for tomorrow.

CHAPTER SIXTEEN

They're freaking out about the film. CALL ME.

The message blared at him, his phone vibrating on the nightstand, his eyes bleary from little sleep. But this was the third time his phone had rattled on the wood. He read it one more time, an emergency text from Flynn. *Shit.*

Grabbing his phone, he scrambled out of bed and down the stairs so as not to wake Julia.

"What's going on?" he asked, stepping out onto the balcony, greeted by the early morning June sun rising in the sky. The hot and muggy days of late spring were coasting into New York. Heat vibrated in the air.

"They're worried that we can't handle the studio. That we're not big enough," Flynn said, his voice shaky.

"That's crazy. I've dealt with that studio many, many times. So have you."

"I know," Flynn said, exasperated. "And they were fine with it from the start. But now I think they're getting nervous. I'm worried they're going to back out. I have a breakfast meeting with them in thirty minutes on the Upper West Side."

Clay didn't stop to consider the sleeping woman in his bed, or whether she'd be annoyed that he had to take off. All he could focus on was making sure this film deal went through. Flynn had busted his ass to land the Pinkertons, and if they needed to have egos smoothed or cold feet made toasty, it was his job to do so. The bottom line rested with him.

"I'll be there. Text me the location."

"Thanks man, I need you," Flynn said, relief loud and clear across the phone line.

He headed inside, walked quietly past a sleeping Julia, curled up on her side with her red, flaming hair spread across the white pillowcase, looking like a goddess. His goddess. And he was going to have to tell her what he'd done before they met Charlie.

He showered and dressed quickly, and she snoozed the entire time, barely moving. He imagined she was in the most peaceful land of dreams, finally sleeping easily now that the price tag was off her head.

At least he'd been able to do that for her.

He bent down to softly kiss her cheek. She sighed lightly, but didn't wake. Gently, he shook her shoulder. He was greeted with an inhale, and an exhale. "Julia," he whispered.

Her eyelids fluttered. "Hi," she said, opening them briefly.

"I need to go. I have to meet Flynn and the Pinkertons," he said, glancing at his watch. "Should last an hour. Two, tops. I'll meet you at ten thirty and then we'll see Charlie together."

She nodded sleepily. "Call me at ten, so I can shower?"

"Of course. Don't go without me."

"Do I look stupid?"

"Sassy from the moment she wakes up," he said, shaking his head in amusement.

"Back to sleepy time for me," she said, roping her arms around his neck. "But first. *This*."

She pressed a sweet kiss to his lips. "I love you," she murmured, and his heart thumped painfully against his chest, lurching toward her. He desperately wanted to stay, to sit her down, and to explain. She'd forgive him. Of course she would, right? But he also had made a promise to Flynn and to himself that he'd take care of business. He had time for both. He could manage both. He'd tell her before they met Charlie. "Can we go shopping later for new towels?"

"You don't like my towels?"

She shook her head. "I like big, fluffy ones."

"Then let's get you some big, fluffy towels."

"And I kind of think you could use a more comfortable bench on your balcony. Those wooden slats are hard."

"Considering what I will do to you on that, let's get it today."

She smiled again. "My flight's at three."

"Then we will shop or we won't shop, but whatever we do I will love every second of it because I'll be with you, and I love you so much," he said. "And if I could blow this off and spend the morning inside you, I would. Believe me."

Believe me. His words echoed. He needed her to believe him.

"It's okay. Soon, we'll have plenty of Sunday mornings to be lazy and naughty together."

"Lazy and naughty. Gorgeous, that is a promise."

He'd keep that promise. He would absolutely keep that promise.

* * *

Coffee. She needed coffee, stat. Her brain was fuzzy and her muscles were sluggish, and the late-night poker and even later-night sex had worn her out. After a quick shower, she grabbed her clutch purse and her phone, and headed downstairs. She didn't bother hunting out coffee in the kitchen. She was a coffee-shop kind of woman, and besides, she really should get to know the cafes in this neighborhood. It was going to be *her* neighborhood soon, and that prospect brought a grin to her face as she pressed the down button in the elevator.

Her elevator.

Her lobby.

She couldn't believe she'd said yes so quickly, so easily to his question. She should be terrified of packing up and moving across the country. She should hem and haw, and think and consider. But as she pushed open the door of *their* building, stepping out into the bright morning sun on *their* block, she knew.

There was no question about it.

She and Clay were more than solid. They had a future, a bright and beautiful, smart and seductive future. He was her match; he was the one she hadn't been looking for, but who had found his way to her regardless. He was the one she couldn't imagine being without. To think they'd started as a one-night stand, and now they'd become . . . well, they'd become indispensable to each other.

As she ordered her coffee—black with room for cream—she considered that it might be a risk moving here with him. She could get hurt. She could be left. Worst of all, she could be played like a fool.

And yet, this was Clay, and he wasn't that kind of a man. He'd be more likely to travel to Pluto than to play her. Maybe love made you take chances, or maybe real love made you take the right chances.

She poured cream in the coffee, knowing he was the right chance.

She left the cafe and ran a finger over her right breast. Not because she had a hankering for self-booby love, but to double-triple check that the money for Charlie was still tucked safely in her bra and ready to turn over. Safe and sound, and nestled against her.

Her phone buzzed, and she pulled it from her purse.

On my way. Be there in ten minutes. Love you.

She couldn't help but smile because he couldn't stop saying *I love you.*

Her stomach rumbled, a reminder she hadn't had much dinner last night. The restaurant where they were meeting Charlie was one block away, but she wasn't going to show up early to eat and risk running into Charlie alone just because her tummy was growling. She was a big girl and could withstand hunger. Besides, once they were through with the mobster she was planning on ordering French toast with butter and syrup, and enjoying every single bite. She texted back, letting Clay know she was parked outside the cafe at a tiny little sidewalk table.

She sank down in a metal chair, took a drink of her coffee and scanned the block that would soon become second nature to her. With her sunglasses on, she watched the world of the West Village go by on a Sunday morning, checking out hip families with young children racing ahead of them, surveying couples draped over each other, guys and guys, girls and girls, girls and guys, then an inked young man heading to a tattoo shop across the street called No Regrets. *Great name for a tattoo parlor*, she thought, as he entered, probably to add to his markings.

Her phone rang, and it was a 917 number she didn't recognize, so she answered in case Clay was borrowing Flynn's phone. Maybe his cell had died.

"Hello?"

"Hey, Julia! It's Liam. I hope I didn't catch you at a bad time."

She leaned back and smiled. "Nope. Just enjoying this gorgeous June morning in Manhattan."

"That was a fun game last night. You play fierce."

"Why, thank you. I rather enjoyed taking your money from you. Perhaps we'll be able to play more. Seems I might be moving to Manhattan," she said, and if she could bottle this feeling—happiness, hope, possibility—and sell it, she'd be rich. Because everyone should want to feel this way. Effervescent.

"You are shitting me," he said.

She laughed. "Why would I joke about that?"

"Because I was going to ask you if there's any way you'd consider being my bartender at Speakeasy. That drink you made last night was amazing."

"Well, you're easy, then, if I sold you on one drink," she said, figuring he was joking.

"I'm serious, Julia. Your drink was to-die for, and you also have the right attitude that I want behind the bar. Tough, but friendly. Playful, but not flirty. Smart, but inviting."

Pride bloomed in her chest. Her luck was changing. She was coming out ahead based on skills, not looks. She was landing options in life, rather than having them taken away from her. Her future was unfurling before her like a smooth open road, the top thrown down and the radio blasting. "Tell me more about the job," she said, and Liam shared details on the pay, the timing, and his plans.

"Sounds interesting," she said, playing it cool. "But I do already own a successful bar in San Francisco. I'm a little beyond the just-a-bartender level. I'm not that interested in working for someone when I can work for myself."

"I could even offer you an ownership stake if you'd like," he said.

"Let me think about it and get back to you. I'll have to see what my lawyer thinks," she said playfully.

"We have the same one. Let's hope he has the same interests."

"In any case, I am honored you asked. I'll get back to you soon."

She hung up and shook her head, amazed at how this treasure map was revealing itself. And there, in the middle of it all, inside the chest weren't gems or rubies, but the most precious gift of all—a real love. She was a lucky woman, and this could be her life, here in the Village in New York.

She returned to her people watching. A pretty woman in a little black dress and high heels yawned as she passed Julia, likely wearing last night's clothes. She wondered how many of these people were neighbors, and if she'd soon get to know the gentleman who owned the cafe, or the guy across the street walking a pug, or this fellow in the black suit coming into view.

But when she looked up to see the face of the man strolling past her, her heart plummeted six feet underground. Then burrowed even farther when the man stopped, his muddy brown eyes on her, his dark hair freshly combed, his suit neatly pressed.

"Red. Fancy meeting you here."

The voice was an icicle on her skin.

She swallowed back her fear. Nothing to be afraid of. She had his money. That's all he wanted, anyway. Even if Clay wasn't here to protect her. He'd be here any minute, and besides, she could handle *this*.

Charlie crooked his arm at a right angle and looked at his watch. "I am early for our pointless meeting, but I will join you anyway," he said, pulling out the chair next to her.

"Pointless?"

"So pointless," he said with a bored sigh. "Except for the handshake part."

She kept her face stony and impassive, but her mind was whirring. She had no clue what he was hinting at. She didn't plan on letting on, though. One more time with the poker face for Charlie, because he didn't deserve her emotions.

She reached into her bra, and took out the bills. "I have what you wanted, and I believe this means we are through."

He gave her a look as if she were an idiot child, and waved her off. "We are all good," he said, raising his hand dismissively.

Her eyebrows shot up. Forget hiding her reaction now. "What do you mean?" she asked, as a cab screeched to a stop. "You suddenly decided to forgive my debt?"

He scoffed at her. "That is funny. But I am not a forgiving man. He paid me. Your lawyer. Good man. Better than that ex-boyfriend of yours," Charlie said, stopping to scratch behind his ear. Julia's jaw dropped. She was sure she was hearing things. He couldn't possibly have said just that. "Dillon Whittaker always seemed a little shifty to me. I hear he's peddling island real estate."

But the words about Dillon didn't register, because she was still reeling from the blow. It was as if she'd been punched out of nowhere. A jab to the right. A hit to the left. Her head was spinning, and she was seeing stars.

Then she was seeing Clay. Standing next to her, fists clenched at his sides, staring at Charlie. "We weren't supposed to meet until eleven," he said to Charlie through gritted teeth.

"I was out for a stroll since this is such a lovely neighborhood, and look who I ran into," he said, gesturing to Julia. "Lucky me. I got to spend to spend a few minutes with her. She even tried to pay me. But I had to tell her the matter was already settled between men."

It was as if a truck had slammed into her, smashing everything in her body.

Clay looked at Julia, and she saw it in his eyes. Guilt. He was cloaked in it. He reeked of it.

"Clay," she began slowly, but her brain was quickly lining up the pieces, and she had a sickening feeling that she knew what he'd done. "Charlie says— "

He cut her off. "I can explain," he said, sitting next to her, reaching for both her hands and clasping them in his.

"What do you have to explain? The fact that you paid him already?" she said heavily, the words like tar in her mouth. She hoped she'd heard wrong. She prayed that Charlie was lying. He was a liar, right? That was a more likely explanation than that her man had lied to her.

He closed his eyes briefly, and the shame washed over his features. It was evident in his mouth, in his eyes, in his jaw. "It was all a fake? The game was rigged?"

Clay shook his head adamantly. "No, the game wasn't rigged. It was all real. I swear."

"Then why doesn't he need the money I won? Is it true you paid him already?" Her heart, so full of hope and joy, was turning black, like it had been painted over with a brush, becoming dark and cold in seconds.

"I paid him yesterday," he said, grasping her hand tighter. But she shook him off, tears threatening to spill down her face as that word—*yesterday*—rang in her ears. The only thing that stopped the waterworks was the presence of Charlie. She bit her tongue so she wouldn't cry in front of that man. "I did it because I love you. Because I needed you safe."

"When? When yesterday did you pay him?"

His jaw tensed. "Last night."

"But when last night?"

"During the game."

"When?" she asked once more time. Biting out the word. "It. Matters. When?"

"He called earlier in the day, and said he needed it by midnight," Clay said. Julia was used to Charlie's capriciousness, to the way he changed up times and dates and deadlines to suit himself. This was Charlie's M.O. "And you were losing, and I didn't know if you were going to pull it off," he said, and his words cut her to the quick. "So I wired him the money."

"Answer the question, Clay. When exactly did you wire him the money?"

Clay looked as if stones were in his mouth. "Around eleven-thirty."

"After I told you I loved you?"

He nodded.

"After our conversation about Michele?"

Another nod, followed by a heavy sigh.

"After you told me you were texting Flynn about the Pinkertons?"

"Yes."

"Were you texting Flynn or Charlie?"

He looked down, and in his silence she knew his answer, and it ripped through her body like a painful tear, like invisible hands were shredding her to pieces.

A loud scraping sound met her ears. Charlie had pushed back his chair. "As fascinating as it is to witness a lover's quarrel, I have business matters to attend to. Mr. Nichols, I thank you very kindly for securing the transaction last night so that I could get on my flight to Miami. I have business to attend to there. I believe the final term of our deal was a handshake," he said offering his hand to Clay. The two men shook and Julia wanted to bite both of their fingers, leaving teeth marks, and making them both yelp. Charlie patted Julia on the shoulder. "And that means, Red, you are free and clear. It has been a pleasure working with you. You made it entertaining for me, and I will miss my top ringer. But I will surely find someone else who owes me soon. Enjoy Cubic Z. I will not be drinking there again," he said. That was what she wanted, what she'd been fighting for, and she somehow knew Charlie meant every word. There was honor among thieves. His word was good on this matter.

He walked off, leaving Julia alone with the man who'd played her. "I don't understand. You think this is okay because you did it for love?"

"No. Yes," he said, his voice wobbly as he shoved his hand through his hair. "*Yes*. Julia, I didn't want anything to happen to you, so I got him the money."

She softened for a moment, because she understood some part of his actions. Deeply and truly. "I get that. I honestly do. I understand you wanted to protect me, and I don't fault you for that. Because I'd have done the same for you, and I'm okay with that," she said, dropping her hand on top of his. Relief flooded his eyes when she made contact. But it was short-lived because she took her hand away, placing them both in her lap. Her anger stole all the softness, replacing it with only the sharp, cruel betrayal she felt. "But I don't understand why the hell you didn't tell me. It's been twelve hours since you sent him the money. You had so many chances to tell me that the rules of the game had changed."

She watched him swallow hard, a terribly pained look in his eyes. "I wanted to tell you."

"But you didn't. You let me play the end of the game thinking it mattered. I was losing, and you told me to go back in there and kick ass, knowing it didn't matter how I played. You sent me back to play a game that was, for all intents and purposes, rigged. Because it didn't matter what I did," she said, her voice threatening to break. "That's the moment, Clay. Then.

There. On the street. After you told me you loved me. That's when you needed to tell me about Charlie's new deadline. I'd have understood completely if you pulled me aside and said, 'Hey gorgeous, bad news,'" she said, dropping her voice to imitate a man's deeper tones, "'Charlie called and we need to get him the money now.' That's *all* you had to say. That's it."

"I know. I should have. But you were happy and determined, and I wanted you . . ." He let his voice trail off.

"You wanted me to believe I could do it," she supplied.

"Yes," he said with a heavy sigh.

"You wanted me to think I'd pulled it off myself. But I only wanted one thing. To not be played. And you took that away from me. You, of all people, should know better. You hate lies and you hate liars, and you lied to me by *not* telling me. You patted me on the ass and sent me into a game that didn't matter, but you led me to believe it did. Then I won and I practically danced down the street afterwards, and you kissed me and told me you were proud of me. I thanked you for making it possible for me to win on my own terms. And that was another moment that you could have told me."

She stopped to grab him by the arm, trying to make her point. "Instead, you let me believe I'd won my freedom," she said, and now the lump in her throat was so painful that it felt like a swollen ache. She brought her hand to her mouth, as if she could keep the crying at bay. But one rebel tear streaked down her cheek as she whispered, "Then you made love to me in your house, in front of the mirror, and asked me to move in with you. And you *knew* then. All you had to do was tell me. I would have still said yes."

"I wanted you to be happy. And I didn't know how to say it," he said, trying to reach for her, to tug her back in for an embrace, but she held him off.

"You're a goddamn lawyer. You talk to people for a living. Your whole world is semantics and details," she said, the words breaking on her tongue like salty waves. She took a deep breath, trying to somehow settle the tears that threatened to wrack her body. "You could have found a way to tell me. Instead, you spent the whole night telling me you loved me, and asking me to move in, when you should have been telling me the truth. FIRST. Because the truth is fine. The truth isn't what hurts. It's the time you had when you chose to not tell me the truth. And that makes me feel like I gave you my heart and you played me like a fool."

"I only did it to protect you."

"I did something once to protect you. I lied about who you were to protect you," she said, reminding him of that morning on the street in San Francisco when Stevie showed up. Clay winced as she mentioned it. "And what happened? You walked away."

"You've got to understand. I was trying to help you last night, Julia," he said, his words slick with desperation.

"I know your intentions were good, but this isn't about your intentions. It's about your actions, because those matter more to me. I have been deceived so badly over money by men." She grabbed his shirt collar, her eyes locking with his. "I need you, the man I love, to never deceive me. I want to be on your team, but you've got to play fair. I'm fine with what you did, but I am not fine with *how* you did it. I am *not* fine with those twelve hours that you had to tell me the truth. If you had time to ask me to move in with you, you certainly had the time to tell me about Charlie's demands," she said, as she stood up quickly, pushing away from the table.

"Please don't go."

"We are making a scene, and when patrons at my bar make a scene I ask them to leave, and that is what I'm doing," she said as she walked down the street.

He kept pace alongside her. "I am sorry. That is all I can say. I fucked up, and I'm so sorry."

She stopped outside his building, parking her hands on her hips. "Do you know how I feel right now? Do you?"

"Terrible?" he offered up weakly.

"*Stupid.* Like I'm the biggest idiot in the world," she said, erecting a wall inside her to keep the tears locked up. She had to say this. He had to know. "And it makes me feel as if everything that happened between us last night was a lie."

"The way I feel for you is not a lie, Julia," he pleaded, and she could hear every note of his pain. But she hurt too. "It's the truest thing in the world."

"Then you ought to act like that," she said, staring sharply at him as she grabbed the handle of the door.

"So what happens next?"

"I'm leaving New York. And I'm going to go home to my house, and that's as far as I know right now."

"Please. Give me a chance to make this up to you," he said, practically begging.

Once inside the elevator, she placed her hand on his chest. "I understand you want to. But I have to leave for the airport in two hours, I need to pack, and I'm hungry as hell."

"At least let me feed you. Let me get you something to eat."

"If only this were as simple as French fries," she said as they stepped out onto his floor. "But you can help me pack."

"Then I will gladly help you pack," he said, and together they went upstairs, both like beaten-down ragdolls, listless when they should have been joyful. They didn't speak as she gathered her lotion, shampoo and makeup from the bathroom, dropping them into a plastic bag, and layering that on top of her clothes. Maybe there was nothing more to say. The time for words had passed. This wasn't about argu-

216 · LAUREN BLAKELY

ments, or trying to convince someone you were right or wrong. This was about whether she'd listen to her heart or her head, and what both had to tell her.

"So what happens, Julia?" he asked as he zipped her bag. "Are you coming back?"

She met his eyes, the sadness in hers reflected back. "I want to, but I really need to think about everything now. I need a solid week apart. No contact. To make sure I'm not making a mistake. It's easy for you if this doesn't work out. You're not giving up anything. I'm changing everything."

"And I would never take that or you for granted. I promise, I will cherish you, as I already do. Will you let me buy you a ticket to return?"

"You are free to do whatever you want, but I need to be certain that this is right for me. So I can't promise you I'm going to use it. This has been a crazy weekend, from the game, to things ending with Charlie, to you and me. You hurt me, and I need to go home and take some time alone to make sure I'm not being foolish again, Clay."

"You're not," he said, reaching for her hand, clasping it in his. Oh, how she wanted to fall into his arms. Those strong sturdy arms that had protected her, fought for her, held her. But this wasn't about him. It was about her, and whether she could let herself turn so much of her life, and her heart, and her home, over to someone else again. "I swear."

"You asked me to move my life across the country for you and I said yes in a heartbeat. Because I love you. And the whole time you were hiding something from me. And that something makes me feel like a fool," she said, whispering the last words like a eulogy.

To her, it was the worst name in the world she could call herself. Because she'd been there. Oh, had she been there.

* * *

A little while later, she walked to the door, down the stairs, and to the waiting town car that would whisk her to the airport. He'd offered to ride with her but she'd declined, saying it would be too tempting, and she needed not to be tempted in that way.

He held onto that sentiment like a fragile glass globe of hope, clutching it for several minutes on the way downstairs. But then, he knew better. They'd always been good together physically. What was happening between them now was no longer about chemistry. It was about trust, and she needed to know he was a man of his word in all matters. There was no room for anything less. He had to keep all his promises to her, the big ones and the small ones. Life was rarely about the big things; it was usually about the impact—the potentially damaging impact—of the little things.

After the driver stowed her bags in the trunk, Clay reached for her, pulling her in close. She tucked her face in the crook of his neck, her breasts pressed against his chest. He could feel her heart beating against him and he could have stayed there all day. As she broke the embrace, she cupped his cheek with one hand, a soft fingertip tracing his jaw, sending tremors like quicksilver through his body. He would miss her touch; he would miss all of her.

She stood on tiptoes, brushing her soft lips against his, lingering slowly on his mouth. The kind of kiss that stays with you for days. The kind of kiss you never forget.

Because of how it tastes.

Like goodbye.

CHAPTER SEVENTEEN

He clicked on the flight tracker, and watched the black arrow snake across the Midwest. He dropped his head in his hand, and looked back up minutes later, as if the computer would tell him something. As if she'd appear on some futuristic TV screen from the plane, waving, saying he was forgiven.

"It's okay. I know you were just so caught up in loving me that you forgot to tell me," she'd say with a twinkle in her green eyes, then a pretty wink. She'd press her soft lips against the screen and blow him a kiss. "I'll be back," she'd say and the screen would crackle out, like static, fading to black, but everything would be okay and she'd return to him.

Instead, his life was up in the air. Because he'd been an ass. He'd been scared, wanting to secure his future before he faced his present. He, of all people, should have known better. You don't ask someone to sign until you give them all the facts, and spell out the terms.

He'd gone about it the wrong way, thinking that by asking her to move in first, he'd be able to keep her without reservation. But you don't get the girl until you've gotten the girl. And even then you have to put in the effort every single day to keep her. You don't win before you've won. You keep playing, and fighting for love every day.

He reached for the screen, running his index finger across the cartoonish line of her airplane, scurrying her back to San Francisco. Was she sleeping on the plane? Watching a movie? Having a drink? Vodka on the rocks, probably.

Wait.

If she was drinking, it was whiskey.

Whiskey for loneliness.

But then, maybe she wasn't lonely, he figured as he shut his laptop and made his way to the kitchen, opening the cabinet. Maybe she was happy, and toasting with champagne to better days without him. Chatting it up with the random stranger next to her in seat 2B. Sharing her story. Telling the stranger about what an ass Clay had been. They would laugh at him, and he deserved it. Maybe he didn't deserve anything but to have lost her this way.

This foolish way.

He should have taken the chance, and told her when it happened with Charlie's change-up, rather than waiting. Waiting never did anyone any good. When you waited, the world passed you by. Life passed you by. And the love of your life flew in the dark of night over the country, stretching the distance between you to so much more than three thousand miles.

He left the kitchen and opened the door to his balcony, walked to the railing, and stared at the city as he finished his glass, the liquor burning his throat as he wanted it to.

They should have spent those precious last few hours tangled up together. Or having lunch together. Or shopping together. He wasn't even fond of shopping, but he'd have happily taken her anywhere, letting her pick out the towels she wanted, the new bench for the balcony. Hell, she could redecorate the whole house from stem to stern, any way she wanted. They've have shopped, and then wandered through the neighborhood, his arm around her, discovering the places in the Village that would become theirs: a cafe here, a store there. He'd have gotten her worked up at lunch, touching her legs under the table, slipping his fingers under her skirt, driving her so wild he'd have had to pull her into the restroom at a cafe and fuck her against the wall, her legs wrapped around him, certain that she'd be returning to live with him.

Instead, he was left with this loneliness that could have been avoided with a few simple words spoken hours before.

Avoided with the truth.

He held up his glass, cocked his arm, and considered chucking it five stories down to the street below. Cabs and cars streaked by on a Sunday night, and soft jazz music floated up from a few floors below him. Some kind of melancholy John Coltrane song that might as well have been ordered up for him by the gods of regret.

Maybe that's what whiskey was good for. Maybe whiskey was best for regret, because that was all Clay could taste tonight.

He lowered his arm, the glass still in his hand. He wasn't going to make a mess for someone else. He'd somehow have to find a way to clean up the mess he'd made of this love.

He left the balcony, closing the door behind him as if he could seal shut the memories of all they'd done there. But he couldn't. She was everywhere in his home. She was naked on his couch. She was undressing on his stairs. She was laughing joyfully over a gift in his kitchen. She was dancing in his bedroom. She was sleeping peacefully on his bed. She was giving him her most vulnerable *yes* in the bathroom, telling him she'd leave her life in San Francisco for him.

Like a ghost shadowing him, she was everywhere and nowhere.

He returned to the kitchen, dropping the glass into the sink. Turning around, he reached for the whiskey bottle, and tucked it back into the cabinet. But the bottle rattled. He steadied it quickly, then peered in the cupboard to see what had knocked it off-kilter.

An envelope.

He took the envelope, fat and stuffed. His name was on the front, and his stomach dropped when he read the words: "*This belongs to you. Thank you for the loan. I always pay back my debts.*"

But there was no *xoxo*. No secret message to decode that would reassure him she'd be coming back. There was only money, all ten thousand dollars that she'd won, and he'd lost.

* * *

The next day he wasn't any wiser as to whether she'd be returning. He hadn't heard from her: no emails, no calls, only a text to say she'd landed safely. He took some small solace in the safety update, but it truly wasn't enough for him. He wanted all of her. He needed all of her. And he had virtually none.

He'd zombied his way through the day, grateful that the Pinkertons had signed on the dotted line after the emergency soothe session the day before. Warding off that near-fiasco had given him the mental space to manage the bare minimum he needed to get through the contracts and phone calls on his agenda.

He emailed her the ticket back to New York. He'd booked it for two weeks from now, hoping that was fair—a week apart, a week to plan. She replied with a *thank you*.

He checked countless times for messages from her. Each time he'd come up empty.

He scrolled through his emails on the subway home just to make sure he hadn't missed one from her.

After a workout at his boxing gym that left his shoulders sore and his body tired, he still was no closer to knowing whether she was going to need those fluffy towels or not.

The time without her was like a black hole, a vacuum that gnawed away at him. He'd subtract a few years from his life simply for a note that gave him some sense of which way she was leaning. Something, anything to hold onto, to give him purchase. How had it only been twenty-four hours when it felt like a fucking year?

But that was what love does. It changes your perception of everything, of your own capacity for pain, for hope, and most of all—your perception of time. Because now, time was measured by her, by her presence, by her absence, and his relentless desire for her *yes*.

He checked his phone once more on the way home from the gym, like an addict. He was going to wear a hole through the screen with his thumbprint from all the times he'd swiped it. He needed company; he needed someone. He showered and headed uptown, reasoning that if he wasn't going to find an answer from her, he could at least ask questions of someone else.

When he arrived at the building off Park Avenue with the green awning, the doorman buzzed her apartment. "You have a visitor. Clay Nichols is here to see you," the man said, then paused. "Very well."

He hung up.

"She said to come on up," the doorman said, gesturing to the elevator.

Clay hadn't been here in a long time. He hadn't needed to. Now, he did.

When Michele opened the door, she was wearing a tank top and slim jeans, her hair pulled into a high ponytail, showing off her neck.

A neck that he'd once kissed.

He didn't mince words, or bother with preambles.

"Are you in love with me?" he asked as he walked inside.

"I have been for years," she said, as the door closed behind them.

CHAPTER EIGHTEEN

"I've been thinking of new names for cocktails. Well, Craig and I have," Kim offered during a lull in the crowds on Monday night.

"Yeah? Do tell."

"We came up with a whole list of great names while you were out of town."

"Your hubs is usurping my spot as a partner-in-crime?" Julia asked, resting a hip along the bar as she wiped down glasses.

"Ha. Hardly. But he does like to name drinks. Here's what we've got. A shot called the Long, Hard Night. A stiff drink called the One Night Stand. And a variation on the lemon drop martini that we called Lemon Drop Your Panties," Kim said, and the edges of Julia's lips lifted in a smile.

"Great names," she said, then looked away from Kim because all of them—every single one—reminded her of Clay. He'd been her One Night Stand, her Long,

Hard Night, and she'd dropped her panties countless times for him. Every time, he'd risen—no pun intended—to the challenge, stripping her down to the bare essentials of pleasure and desire, and somehow all that desire had morphed into so much more. Into a mad and passionate love. The kind of love that thundered down the road with wild hoofbeats after midnight. Desperate, reckless, and headfirst.

That was the problem. She needed to pull back and analyze. To think. To consider. "Hey, can I ask you a question?"

"Fire away."

"Has Craig ever lied to you about something because he thought it was for the best?"

Kim shot her a quizzical look. "Well, how would I know?"

"I mean something he eventually 'fessed up to," she added.

"Ah, gotcha," Kim said, scrunching up her forehead as she considered the question. Then she thrust her finger in the air. "Yes! He used to tell me he loved my pot roast when we were first dating, and it turned out he really thought it was dry and stringy."

Julia laughed. "Tell the truth, Kim. Is your pot roast dry and stringy?"

Kim threw back her head and chuckled. "Evidently, I make *the* worst pot roast in the entire universe. It's that bad. But you know what?"

"What?"

"Now if he ever bugs me by leaving his dirty socks on the floor, or failing to put the toilet seat down, I just threaten him with my pot roast. Keeps that man in line," she said, straightening her spine like a drill sergeant issuing orders.

A pair of young men in suits sidled up to the bar and Kim turned her attention to them. Julia's mind stayed put on Kim's story and how it had a happy ending. Wasn't that what everyone wanted? A happy ending? But was a pot-roast fib the same as an omission of the truth?

She didn't know, and wasn't sure how to arrive at an answer. Her brain had grown cloudier in the last twenty-four hours, fuzzier with the distance. Had she overreacted? Been too quick to anger? She was a hot-tempered woman. She knew that about herself. But she valued independence more than anything. Even more than love. If she were to give up her independence, her job, her bar, her home, her sister, even her hairdresser, she had to know with the same clarity she had about how to make a kick-ass cocktail that uprooting her whole damn life—like she were picking up a carpet and shaking everything off it, come what may—was as right as right could be.

Come what may.

That was the real risk, wasn't it? Charging head-first into the great unknown. Throwing away the self-protective armor she'd built since Dillon's betrayal, and shedding all her fiery independence for a chance that could flame out and fade away. Living in close quarters could turn the two of them—two strong-willed, stubborn, controlling people—into a collision course for disaster.

Or they could become better together, come what may.

"Hey Kim," Julia called out as her co-worker deposited the drinks to the customers. "I just thought of another name for a drink. Come What May."

"What's in it?"

"Something risky. Something that makes you want to take a chance. What do you think?"

"I think we need to break out our beakers and start mixing," Kim said, bumping her hip against Julia's.

"Ouch, I think you whacked me with your gigantic belly."

"It's a weapon of mass destruction. Beware," Kim said, rubbing her hands over her beach ball-sized stomach as she reached for spirits to test. "Let's start with— "

But Kim's suggestion was cut short by the clearing of a throat. Julia swiveled around to the bar and spotted a familiar face. She couldn't connect a name to the man, or why she knew him, but the older, dapper gentleman was giving her a serious case of déjà vu, and she hoped he'd alleviate it soon.

"Good evening. I was hoping to find Julia Bell," he said, and that didn't help her one bit. In fact, all her instincts told her that he was working for Charlie, or looking for Dillon, or somehow that she was going to be in a heap of trouble again. A fleet of nerves launched inside her, and she could feel the inklings of flight or fight kick in.

"That's me," she answered, calling on her best tough-chick-behind-the-saloon-bar persona.

"We met briefly before," he began, and something about his classy voice tickled her memory. He wasn't one of Charlie's men after all. Charlie's men were rougher around the edges. This man was proper and finished, like a gentlemanly professor. "And you made me the most fantastic drink I've ever had."

Her lips curved up, a smile threatening to break across her face. "Was it my Purple Snow Globe?"

"Indeed it was." He extended a hand to shake. "I'm Glen Mills, and my magazine has been running a search for the best cocktail ever."

Julia took his hand. "And I trust you found that cocktail here at Cubic Z?"

* * *

Clay sank down onto Michele's couch. "Why didn't you ever tell me?"

She flashed a small, sad smile. "Why didn't you ever notice?"

He held out his hands, showing they were empty. "I don't know."

"Did you? Notice, finally?" she asked, and her voice rose, touching some kind of hopeful note as she sat down across from him in a dove gray chair in her apartment.

He shook his head. "No. But then, lately, I haven't been so astute at connecting the dots, in the right time or the right fashion."

"Then how did you figure it out?" she asked, cocking her head curiously.

"I didn't. Julia did. She mentioned it when we went outside during the game."

Michele winced, then dropped her head in her hands. "She must hate me," she muttered.

"No," he said quickly, needing to reassure her. "She doesn't hate you at all. She's not like that. She thinks you are lovely, and smart, and funny," he said, repeating Julia's words from Saturday. "And I happen to agree with her."

Michele raised her face, and rolled her eyes in self-deprecation. "Some good that did."

"Michele," he said gently.

She shook her head several times. "I feel like an idiot."

"Please don't. You're the farthest thing from that. If anyone's the idiot, it's me. I didn't have a clue."

She managed a small laugh. "I wish I could say that's because I was so good at hiding how I felt, but seeing as Julia noticed it instantly and you didn't have an inkling for ten years, I'm going to have to go with you being completely blind to what's in front of you sometimes. I just have to wonder, though, Clay, how could you not tell?"

He raised both shoulders, shrugging. "I've been trying to figure out how I missed it and all I can conclude is this—I care about you so deeply as a friend, and you're Davis's sister, and I feel like the three of us are kind of in the trenches together. Like we've risen up together in our jobs, and we're this great threesome of friends somehow. I guess I only ever saw you that way."

"Let me ask you a question then," she said, taking a deep breath, the look in her eyes one of fierce determination. "If you'd have known how I felt, would it have made a difference anyway?"

He locked eyes with the woman he'd been friends with for so long. With his best friend's sister. With the gal he had drinks with every Thursday night. The person he'd turned to for advice on the woman who had confused him. She was his friend, always had been, and that's how he wanted to keep her. He shook his head, and sighed. "No," he admitted. "I'm sorry."

She held up a hand. "Please," she said firmly. "No pity for me."

"It's not pity."

"I mean it, Clay," she said. "I'm going to be fine. I've been in love with you for ten fucking years, and have managed it. Now it's time I get out of love with you."

He sank deeper into the couch, and breathed out hard. "Why didn't you say something, if you felt that way?"

She closed her eyes briefly, then opened them. Her mouth was set in a firm line. Then she spoke. "I think, deep down, I knew it was unrequited. That even if I told you, I knew that it wouldn't change a thing. That whatever that kiss was about in college was all it was ever going to be, but it did a number on me."

He tilted his head, stared at her as if she were a science project he was in the middle of constructing. "Why? From one kiss?"

"It was the kiss, but most of all, it was you. I thought you were the most handsome man I'd ever met, and smart, and funny, and most of all, you had your act together. You have no idea what my days are like," she said, with a light laugh. "I love my job. But I spend my days with a lot of messed-up people. And you're the least fucked-up person I've ever known. You don't have issues. You don't have baggage. What you see is what you get. For someone who spends all day fixing people, I suppose I really have been longing for someone I didn't have to fix."

"I take it Liam isn't doing it for you?"

"See, that's not fair. How can you be so observant about my feelings for Liam, but so clueless about how I felt for you?"

"Pretty amazing how I can have blinders on about certain things, isn't it?"

"I do like him . . ." she said, then let her voice trail off.

"But?"

"But, it's hard to like someone when you've been focused on someone else."

"I can understand that," he said, since Julia was his whole world.

"You're madly in love with Julia, aren't you?"

"Madly doesn't even begin to cover it. But we really don't have to talk about her," he said softly.

"I'm a big girl. I can handle it. Talk to me."

"I mean it, Michele. I don't want you to be uncomfortable. You need to tell me if it upsets you if I talk about her."

"I survived six hours of poker with you having your hands all over her, and watching that dopey look of love in your eyes the whole time," she said, both teasing and being truthful. "I can handle talking about her. And if I can't, I'll let you know."

He patted the couch. "Sit next to me."

"I don't know if that's such a good idea."

"What, are you going to throw yourself at me? I'm strong. I'll fight you off."

"Oh, gee. Thanks."

"C'mon. We're friends, and hell if I'm letting you go over this."

She moved off the chair and sat next to him on the couch, tentative in the way she folded her legs up under her, keeping a bit of distance. He took her hand, clasped it in his. "I need plenty of fixing. Trust me on that."

"Okay," she said playfully. "You need Dr. Milo again?"

"I always need Dr. Milo, but I also need you to know I think you're an amazing, beautiful person, and you are going to make some man the happiest man on the planet, and you probably won't need to fix him either."

She squeezed his hand, and it felt good, comforting. Like something he didn't want to lose. "But now you need me to fix something, don't you?" she asked, raising an eyebrow.

"You just said you're tired of fixing people all day. I'll be okay."

"I said I don't *want* to fix the man I'm going to be involved with. But I think we've established that we're friends. And besides, I have a feeling—call me crazy—that you might really need my help. You screwed things up with Julia, didn't you?"

He nodded, guilt written all over his face.

"Tell me everything," she said.

He didn't tell her everything. He'd promised Julia to keep her secrets about her debt. But he told Michele enough about what he'd done. "So what do I do? Just wait for her to decide if she'll move to New York for me?"

Michele nodded. "I'm afraid in this situation, patience is going to be a virtue. But I also think you need to find a way to show her that you can fix things. That when a mistake has been made, you can do more than apologize. Show her through your actions, not just your words. Show her you can fix the things that matter to her."

And with blinding clarity, he knew what to do.

CHAPTER NINETEEN

Julia's jaw dropped at the mention of all the zeroes. "That's the size of the prize?"

Glen Mills nodded and said yes, again and again and again.

"I won a contest I didn't even know I was in AND you want to just give me that much money? No strings attached?"

Glen chuckled, and even his laugh sounded proper. "Well, the string attached is we would very much like to offer you a contract to manufacture the drink in conjunction with Farrell Spirits," he said, mentioning the name of one of the world's largest premium drink makers that was home to many top-flight rums, vodkas, gins and whiskeys bottled around the world.

"Oh my God, like those cosmo and mojito mixes you see in grocery stores," Kim said with a shriek.

Julia turned to Kim, and it was like looking in a mirror and seeing a grin as wide as the sea, eyes twinkling, surprise and shock etched across her face. She returned her gaze to the gray-haired gentleman, who'd become something of a Santa Claus. Dropping in unexpectedly, bringing only presents, and a *ho, ho, ho.* But Santa wasn't real, and there had to be some loophole he'd spring on her. The devil lived in the details, and bathed himself in fine print. She rearranged her features, fixing a more serious look on her face. "There has to be some kind of catch? Do I have to give up my bar, or my firstborn, or an arm, maybe?"

Glen laughed, and shook his head. "No, Ms. Bell. We simply want to be in business with you. Farrell Spirits contracted my magazine to embark on a nationwide hunt for the best cocktail and the string attached is that the company would very much like to make it and turn it into a mass-market available product."

Chills raced over her skin, goose bumps of sheer possibility. She didn't know what to do or say. But this must be what it felt like to win the lottery: disbelief of the highest order. "So you want the recipe, of course?"

"We are going to need the recipe if we agree to the terms, but I assure you it will not be printed in the magazine. It would become a trade secret of course, and Cubic Z can remain the only bar where the drink can be made or ordered fresh."

Julia grabbed Kim's arm in excitement. "Do you have any idea what that would do for our business?

It'd go through the roof," she said, now shrieking. "And that'll be so good for you and Craig and the baby."

"I know," Kim said, her face glowing.

"There is one small item though," Glen said, interrupting, and Julia's shoulders fell. This was the moment when the devil revealed himself. There was no such thing as a free lunch. Her life was not *X-Factor with Cocktails*. There would be a catch; there always was.

"Yes?" she asked through a strangled gulp.

"Even if you don't accept the Farrell offer, I will still be writing about this drink in our magazine because it is divine," he said. "And there are no strings attached to that recognition. I would simply be shirking my journalistic duties to do anything less."

Julia's smile returned. "Far be it from me to turn you into a shirker of duties," she said, and extended a hand to shake.

Later that night, when she returned to her home, she couldn't wipe the damn grin off her face if she'd tried. Because for the first time in a long time, she'd won something based on her skills. Sheer talent alone had made this happen. She wasn't saving the world, and she certainly wasn't curing cancer, but she could mix a damn fine drink, and build a damn fine bar, and no man could ever take that away from her.

Funny that she hadn't even known she was a contender, but that made this victory all the sweeter. It was her victory, her prize, and her success. Based on something intrinsic to her that no one, no mobster, no douche of an ex-boyfriend, could ever twist or manipulate.

As she unlocked the door to her home, she was filled with a sense of pride over a job well done.

The only trouble was there was someone she desperately wanted to share this moment with.

She settled for her sister instead. McKenna had just returned from her honeymoon, so Julia called her to tell her the news.

* * *

Three days later, McCoy's was bustling with the usual lunch crowd. This was Midtown Meeting Central, and everyone must have gotten the memo to wear a suit today because the restaurant was packed with sharp-dressed men and women, angling for deals, pitching their wares, hoping to get the person across the table to sign on the dotted line. Clay recognized that hard and hungry look in many of their eyes; he had it himself. Only this time he was hunting out information, and the best purveyor of intel in all of Manhattan was digging into his steak right now.

"Someday I'm gonna charge you, but for now, let me say this is delish, and I will happily take my payment in the form of a meal," Cam said, as he stuffed a forkful into his mouth.

"Like I wasn't going to pick up the tab. And you know I'd pay you in a heartbeat for your services," Clay said as he worked through his pasta dish. "But are you ever planning on telling me what you found out?"

"No. I'm going to eat this steak and run," Cam joked, with his mouth full. He chewed, and then took a long swallow of his dry martini. He subscribed to the notion that steak was meant to be enjoyed properly with spirits, the time of day be damned. It was one of the very many reasons Clay called this man a friend. He was steady, reliable, amusing as hell, and loved to share his special talent of finding anyone or anything with friends, asking only for the cost of a meal.

Picking up the tab was nothing if he could deliver what Clay needed.

Cam wiped his mouth with the cloth napkin, then set down his fork and knife for a break from the food. "I'll put you out of your misery. My guys found him. All those stories Liam was telling about real estate in the Bahamas? You were onto something."

Clay's eyes lit up, and a spark of anticipation ran through him. Could it be this simple? That he'd been found, coincidentally, in the very place where Liam had randomly been asked to buy a condo? "He's in the Bahamas?"

Cam scoffed, and waved a big hand. "No. That'd be too easy. What world do you live in? The land of coincidence? He's not in the Bahamas, but you were right to put all those clues together from what this fucker did. He's taking pictures of homes."

"Exactly what he was doing when he was in San Francisco," Clay added, raising an eyebrow in question.

Clay had supplied Cam with the clues, tracking down every last one Julia had ever told him about her ex. He'd shot homes for realtors. His niche behind the camera was making rooms look much bigger, and Dillon had told Julia on their first date that someday he'd be sipping a drink in the Bahamas. Clay had added up those details, alongside Liam's unexpected recon work, and Charlie's brief comment at the cafe on Sunday, and went with a hunch that Dillon might be in the islands snapping shots for scams.

Cam tapped his nose with his index finger. "Bingo. Because here's the thing about men like that who run scams. They tend to fall back on old habits. They do what works. Whether it's taking pictures, or conning money. And he seems to have gotten in good with some of the scam artists on a certain island, trying to hustle money selling time-share condos that don't really exist. His job is to take the pictures of the one good condo, make them look majestic, and the other guys peddle the properties that don't really exist."

"But where is he?" Clay asked, because that was all that mattered, and he damn near wanted to cross his fingers with hope, but he wasn't a finger crosser. He was a man who knew the law, and knew that when you ran afoul of it there were certain islands where it was better or worse for you to be.

He hoped to hell that Dillon was in one of those countries that would be worse for Dillon.

"Can you say Montego Bay? Because if you can, I've got the address for where Dillon Whittaker is living now," Cam said, and slapped a piece of paper on the table.

Clay grinned, a pure, wicked grin broke across his face as he picked up paper. "God bless Jamaica and its fine extradition laws with the United States of America. Looks like someone is going to need to pay the taxman."

Taxes were a bitch.

* * *

"So what's your verdict?"

"Uncross your legs," Gayle said.

"I hardly think uncrossing my legs is the answer to all my romantic woes," Julia said after telling her stylist most of the details of her situation.

Gayle winked at her in the mirror as Julia followed orders. "I don't know, sweetie. Kinda sounds like uncrossing your legs has been working pretty well for you with this guy."

Julia laughed. "Fine, you got me on that."

"Champion race horse in the sack, right?"

She covered her mouth with her hand daintily, pretending to be shocked. "Did I say that?"

"No. But it sure as hell sounds like it, from the stories you've told me about his prowess."

"Prowess doesn't even begin to cover it. But that's not what we're talking about. I need to know what you think I should do next. A woman can't make this kind of decision without consulting her stylist."

"Don't consult me," Gayle said, brandishing her silver scissors playfully in the mirror.

"Consult the scissors?"

Gayle shook her head. "Ask the ink," she said, and tapped her bare arm with the silver scissors, pointing to the cursive letters on her arm spelling out *I want to be adored.* Julia had always admired the tattoo, even more so because Gayle's wish for love had come true. Julia leaned in close to the tattoo and whispered, as if offering a plaintive plea to an oracle. "Ink, what should I do?"

"Allow me to translate for the ink," Gayle said as she resumed snipping hair. "Do you love him?"

"Yes."

"Can you forgive him?"

When phrased like that, the answer seemed patently obvious. "Yes," she admitted in a small voice.

"And most of all, does he adore you?"

Julia tried to suppress a smile, as if she could hold in all that she felt by not admitting the pure and honest truth. But she blurted it out anyway. "So much."

Gayle gave her an approving nod. "One more question. Do you have any idea how devastated I will be to no longer do your hair if you move to New York? Fortunately, I still go there every few months to cut Jane Black's hair," she said, mentioning the Grammy-winning rock singer.

"Name-dropper."

"I'll see if I can squeeze you in after Ms. Black."

"Watch it. I'm going to be famous now, too. You'll have to start calling me Ms. Purple Snow Globe."

"You do know that sounds like the name of a vibrator, right?"

"Which makes it an even better name for a drink. Because when you drink one, it makes you feel like a vibrator does," Julia said, and cracked herself up, along with her stylist.

"That should be the marketing slogan. But you don't need a vibrator with your champion racehorse."

"*If* I take him back," Julia added, emphasizing that one word. *If.* Because she had promised herself a week to make this decision.

Gayle rolled her eyes. "A woman's stylist always knows."

* * *

All night Julia was tempted to text Clay. To let him know what happened with Farrell Spirits. To tell him which way she was leaning. But she also knew she needed to give this a week. The time apart was less about him, and more about her. It was about what she wanted in life, but more so, what she needed. As the days had passed with necessary silence, her heart had become clearer. She trusted him. She'd become sure of that. The question remained, though–did she trust herself? Did she have enough faith in her own gut to make the right choice when it came to men? When it came to love?

As she settled into bed, she glanced at the clock on her nightstand. It blared one-thirty in garish red. Tomorrow would be Saturday, and her self-imposed Clay exile was nearing an end. Only twenty-four more hours until she gave him her answer.

She reached for her phone so she could reply to McKenna. She and her sister had been texting earlier in the day about getting together for a Saturday girls' lunch. She hadn't seen her sister since the wedding, and she missed her something fierce.

"See you at noon, and get ready for a tackle-hug, because that's what I'll be giving you," she typed.

Her sister replied seconds later. "You better get ready to receive one too."

That left Julia with a big, fat smile. Then she clicked over to her email for one final check before bed, and her heart stopped when she saw his name. The email had been sent a few hours earlier in the evening, and she was only seeing it now. Part of her wanted to berate him, to tell him to give her the space she'd asked for. But mostly, she felt giddy. She missed that man, and the happiness over simply seeing his name in her email was a potent reminder, like someone had underlined it with yellow highlighter, of what she should do.

from: cnichols@gmail.com
to: purplesnowglobe@gmail.com
date: June 7, 10:48 PM
subject: For You

Julia,

I've seen enough movies to know that when it comes to romance, the man usually screws up and then makes some sort of big gesture for the woman. The boom box in the rain, the trip to the top of the Empire State Building, or sometimes just flowers, candy, or a note. But you're not that kind of a woman—the kind who needs or wants flowers, candy, or a note. Though I'll gladly give you all of that if you let me. But I want to make good on a promise I made to you at your sister's wedding. I spend my days helping my clients to make more money and to protect their interests. But I can protect you too. And I can give you something I know matters more to you than flowers, candy, or a note. Because I know you, Julia. I know you so well. And what I can do is this—I can right a wrong for you. Please click on the link and you'll see.

She hovered over the blue link, without a clue what she would find. She tapped it, bringing up a small blog called *Death and Taxes*. Julia eyed it curiously at first, then the possibility slammed into her of what he'd done. Some kind of wild hope bloomed in her chest as she scrolled through the short, succinct blog posts, each one detailing a tax-evading citizen who'd been caught. Then she found the one that had her name written all over it.

California resident Dillon Whittaker has been served with an extradition order from Jamaica back to the United States where he is currently under investigation for failing to pay taxes on $100,000 in income from the previous year. The IRS said it learned of Mr. Whittaker's non-compliance with the tax code under its Whistleblower Law that encourages tipsters to turn in tax cheats by bringing forth evidence on potential tax evasion to the IRS. If the information is substantive enough, the individual may receive a portion of the back taxes paid by the tax evader. We will continue to report on the outcome of the investigation into Dillon Whittaker. Sources tell us jail time is coming soon.

Julia leapt out of bed and shouted victoriously, pumping a fist in the air. She brought her phone to her lips, kissing the screen over and over. She was sure she'd soon take flight, and rocket around the city on this crazy glee she felt. "Take that, fucker."

She'd never realized how sweet revenge would taste, but it tasted fucking spectacular, especially when she clicked back to her email and read the last line from Clay. *I had my friend track him down in Jamaica, and I called the IRS to turn him in.*

The only thing that tasted better was the next note from Clay. A separate email, also sent a few hours ago. She only noticed it after she stopped dancing on her bed. She dropped back down to the mattress and read more of his words.

from: cnichols@gmail.com
to: purplesnowglobe@gmail.com
date: June 7, 10:52 PM
subject: You

Just remember this, for what it's worth. I adore you. Absolutely, completely, with everything I have. I will give you everything, all my heart, all my love, anything you want. You mean more to me than I ever imagined. Being without you is hell.

Without thinking, she clicked over to her texts to call up his number and ring him, but the reflection of the red numbers in the mirror stopped her. It was after one in the morning here, so it was the middle of the night in New York. He'd be sound asleep. But someone else she knew and loved was wide awake. Someone who knew a little something about big gestures herself.

She called McKenna, who answered immediately. "It's late. Are you okay?"

"Everything is perfect. Or it's going to be after I see you. I'm on my way over."

CHAPTER TWENTY

Her back was smashed against the Qbert machine, and her hands were raised in front of her face. McKenna had landed another punch to the ribs, then one to her shoulder. And now, it was coming: the noogie. Her sister grabbed her hair, and dug her knuckles into Julia's head.

"Don't ever, ever, ever do that again!"

"Okay, okay, okay," Julia said, relenting for the twentieth time.

McKenna backed off, huffing. "I would have helped you," she said, her eyes on fire with frustration. "I would have given you the freaking money like that." She snapped her fingers in emphasis. "That's why you deserve to be beaten up. You're supposed to let your big sister help you."

"I know, McKenna. Trust me, I know," she said, placing her hand on her heart. "But I had to keep you safe. Don't you get it? I love you and I love Chris, and I'd do anything to protect your happiness."

"Including not telling me a frigging mobster had a price tag on your head and was waving guns in your face?"

Julia lifted her shoulders casually. "Technically, the gun was never waved at me."

McKenna pushed her hands roughly through her blond hair. "I'm soooo mad at you. I love you so much, and if anything had happened to you and I could have solved the problem, I would have died. Do you know that? Died! Like this," McKenna said, then flopped down on the floor, and played dead for effect. Ms. Pac-Man trotted over and licked McKenna's face.

She craned her neck up at Julia. "See? Do you feel bad now? I would have been dead without you, and my dog would be sad."

Julia kneeled down and offered a hand, pulling McKenna to a sitting position. McKenna flung her arms around Julia's neck. She'd always been prone to theatrics. "Promise me," her sister said, "that if you ever get in a pickle with the mob again you will come to me right away, and I will pay whatever you need."

Julia laughed, but nodded into her sister's hair. "Promise."

"Pinky swear?"

"Pinky swear," she said as they twisted their little fingers together. "But, um, that's not actually why I came here."

McKenna rolled her eyes. "I know. You need my special touch, and I know just how to pull this off. But I'm paying for it, and there are no ifs, ands, or buts about it."

"Fine. But only because you want to."

"And we're going to need Chris's help."

"Somebody call my name?" Chris said, walking bleary-eyed down the hall, wearing only his lounge pants.

"Did you actually wake up when I said your name?" McKenna asked.

"No," he said, rubbing his hand against his eyes. "I'm pretty sure it was the '*Don't ever do that again*' screeching that rousted me at three in the morning."

"We need your help."

"Is this another crazy scheme of yours, McKenna?" he asked arching an eyebrow.

"Yes, but it's in the name of love, and isn't love worth everything?"

He looped his arms around his wife and planted a kiss on her cheek. She leaned into it, and smiled. Julia didn't feel jealous. Not one bit. She had that in her life. Waiting for her on the other side of the country. "Of course," he said.

* * *

"I'm going to miss you so much," Julia said.

"I'm going to miss you too. But we'll see each other."

"We will."

"And don't worry about a thing. I'll take care of everything. Every-single-thing. Now go."

Julia wrapped her sister in one final hug, and then said goodbye as the sun rose over San Francisco.

from: purplesnowglobe@gmail.com
to: cnichols@gmail.com
date: June 8, 9:45 AM
subject: You too

I would have called you last night when I read your note, but it was one-thirty in the morning my time, and I didn't want to wake you up. But I was over the moon! I literally danced on my bed, and screamed with happiness. Does that make me an awful witch for celebrating a man's potential incarceration? I hope not. And I can't think of a better present. Well, I **can** think of a better present . . .

from: cnichols@gmail.com
to: purplesnowglobe@gmail.com
date: June 8, 6:47 AM
subject: Late-night calls

Did I somehow give you the impression I would be unreceptive to a middle of the night call from you? I'd answer anytime. Be ready anytime. I am always ready.

from: purplesnowglobe@gmail.com
to: cnichols@gmail.com
date: June 8, 10:12 AM
subject: Ready or not?

I didn't want to be rude and wake you up. But what you did is amazing. I can't believe you found him. Wait. I can believe it. You are some kind of master fixer.

from: cnichols@gmail.com
to: purplesnowglobe@gmail.com
date: June 8, 7:27 AM
subject: Call me Mr. Fix-It

I can fix things around the house too. I am very good with my hands.

from: purplesnowglobe@gmail.com
to: cnichols@gmail.com
date: June 8, 10:52 AM
subject: Yes. You are.

I believe I am well acquainted with your manual dexterity.

from: cnichols@gmail.com
to: purplesnowglobe@gmail.com
date: June 8, 8:01 AM
subject: Come again

You should get reacquainted with it.

from: purplesnowglobe@gmail.com
to: cnichols@gmail.com
date: June 8, 11:20 AM
subject: Your note from last night . . .

So . . . this whole adoration thing . . . are we talking pedestal, shrine or just overall worship level?

from: cnichols@gmail.com
to: purplesnowglobe@gmail.com
date: June 8, 8:31 AM
subject: More than worship

You are adored on every level. I can't even joke about it because it's all too true.

from: purplesnowglobe@gmail.com
to: cnichols@gmail.com
date: June 8, 11:48 AM
subject: Exciting news!

I won a contest for my Purple Snow Globe!

from: cnichols@gmail.com
to: purplesnowglobe@gmail.com
date: June 8, 9:07 AM
subject: As you predicted the night I met you

Tell me more.

from: purplesnowglobe@gmail.com
to: cnichols@gmail.com
date: June 8, 12:32 PM
subject: Be my attorney

Big drink company offered me a contract. I might need a lawyer to look at the fine print.

from: cnichols@gmail.com
to: purplesnowglobe@gmail.com
date: June 8, 9:48 AM
subject: Waiving my fee

I'll do it for you. You can pay me in blow jobs.

from: purplesnowglobe@gmail.com
to: cnichols@gmail.com
date: June 8, 1:05 PM
subject: My kind of payday

I'd give you those for free.

from: cnichols@gmail.com
to: purplesnowglobe@gmail.com
date: June 8, 10:23 AM
subject: Mine too

I want more.

from: purplesnowglobe@gmail.com
to: cnichols@gmail.com
date: June 8, 1:33 PM
subject: Restrained

I'd give you more anyway. Maybe you can tie me up, tie me down, or tie me all around.

from: cnichols@gmail.com
to: purplesnowglobe@gmail.com
date: June 8, 10:52 AM
subject: Bound and Tied

Don't tease me. You know I love the way you look in my ties.

from: purplesnowglobe@gmail.com
to: cnichols@gmail.com
date: June 8, 2:16 PM
subject: Yes to both

I'm not teasing.

from: cnichols@gmail.com
to: purplesnowglobe@gmail.com
date: June 8, 11:28 AM
subject: Yes you are

You've never been a tease. Except when you tease.

from: purplesnowglobe@gmail.com
to: cnichols@gmail.com
date: June 8, 2:44 PM
subject: This is not teasing.

I miss you like crazy.

from: cnichols@gmail.com
to: purplesnowglobe@gmail.com
date: June 8, 3:07 PM
subject: Fix for that

I have a pill you can take that cures that. It's called *come live with me.*

from: purplesnowglobe@gmail.com
to: cnichols@gmail.com
date: June 8, 3:49 PM
subject: Question

How much do you adore me?

from: cnichols@gmail.com
to: purplesnowglobe@gmail.com
date: June 8, 4:02 PM
subject: Answer

So much I can't measure it.

from: purplesnowglobe@gmail.com
to: cnichols@gmail.com
date: June 8, 4:11 PM
subject: And another

How much do you love me?

from: cnichols@gmail.com
to: purplesnowglobe@gmail.com
date: June 8, 4:18 PM
subject: Hit me with another

More than I know what to do with.

from: purplesnowglobe@gmail.com
to: cnichols@gmail.com
date: June 8, 4:20 PM
subject: One more

How happy would you be if I said yes to your offer?

from: cnichols@gmail.com
to: purplesnowglobe@gmail.com
date: June 8, 4:25 PM
subject: One word

Immeasurably.

Iron. He'd cloaked himself in iron. He'd resisted. He hadn't asked for an answer. He hadn't pressured her. He'd simply kept up the volley, letting her lead as she seemed to need at the moment. He held tight to his phone, keeping it on his lap as he worked through the latest set of papers for the Pinkertons from home.

He'd hoped to catch a movie with Davis, since his friend was back in town after working in London for the last few months. But Chris had called him that morning, telling him he was sending a bottle of vintage scotch over as a thank you for his new contract.

"The delivery guys said they'll be there between four and five, so I guess you can just have the doorman sign for it if you're out?"

"I don't have a doorman, but it's not a problem. I've got things I can take care of at the house, so I'll sign for it myself."

"Thanks, man," Chris had said. "It's the least I can do. You rocked the hell out of my new deal."

"If you're pleased, I'm pleased."

But it was four-thirty and the scotch hadn't arrived yet. He was looking forward to it, but not as much as he was looking forward to another note from Julia.

The clock was ticking, lurching towards midnight. If he were a betting man, he'd put money on Julia using up every second of her week of thinking, and giving him the verdict when the clock struck twelve. That would be fine by him. She was worth waiting for.

He scanned the page in front of him when the message light dinged on his phone.

from: purplesnowglobe@gmail.com
to: cnichols@gmail.com
date: June 8, 4:32 PM
subject: One question

Do you still love surprises?

Before he could reply, his phone buzzed with a text message.

Balcony.

He closed his eyes briefly, a spark racing through him with the possibility. Was she reminiscing about the things they'd done on the balcony or was there more to it? He stood up, walked to the door and slid it open. With his heart in his throat and hope winding its way through his bones, he crossed the distance to the railing, and looked down.

His heart stopped, and then started again, thumping hard against his chest with desire, happiness, and mad love.

She was the most beautiful sight in the world. But it wasn't the stockings and the heels, the skirt or the little tank top. It wasn't even her hair falling in waves along her shoulders. It was the two humongous suitcases, one on each side of her. She waved at him as his phone rang.

"My driver left me here on the sidewalk with all my things. Don't suppose you know a big strong man who could help me carry them upstairs to my new home?"

He grinned like a crazy man. "As a matter of fact, I do."

Within seconds—okay, maybe a minute—he was downstairs, looking both ways, and sprinting across the street to her. He gathered her in his arms, and it was like coming home. Her body melted into his as she roped her arms around his neck, and they kissed, and they kissed, and they kissed.

Finally, they pulled apart, but neither one let go. He needed to hold her. To feel her. To know she was real. He ran his hands along her bare arms. The feel of her skin was some kind of magic. He bent his head to her neck, inhaling her scent, the delicious, intoxicating smell of the woman he craved in every way. He lifted a hand to her hair, threading his fingers around her gorgeous flames. The sound of her sweet happy sigh was a shot of pure joy to his heart. She was here. She'd said yes.

"I made sure my flight had Wi-Fi so I could surprise you. Did you think I was in San Francisco the whole day? The time on my laptop was set to Pacific until I landed."

He nodded. "I did, and I take it there's no vintage scotch arriving between four and five?"

"I'm the vintage scotch. I hope you like your surprise."

"You taste better than any scotch, than anything I've ever had to eat or drink. So you're here to stay?" he asked, needing to hear it from her.

She nodded. "I'm here to stay."

"No more running."

"No more running," she repeated.

"We're together."

"Absolutely."

"Which reminds me . . . it's been a week."

She wiggled her eyebrows. "Why do you think I wore a skirt?"

A bolt of pure lust slammed through his body. "Fuck me now," he said, pushing a hand through his hair.

"That's sort of the plan," she said, tipping her forehead to the door to his building. *Their* building.

"Get inside," he growled, lifting a heavy suitcase in each hand. She grinned seductively and strutted across the street, glancing behind to watch him watching her. So perfect, so sexy, so beautiful for him. Once inside the elevator, he pressed the button for the fifth floor.

She reached past him, and hit the stop button. "We're not getting off 'til we get off."

He shook his head appreciatively. "You are my woman. You always have been. You always will be," he said, then reached under her skirt, pulled her panties down and slid his fingers across her. She was ready, oh so ready.

She was eager too, judging from how quickly her nimble little fingers had unzipped his jeans. "You did miss me," he said playfully.

"So fucking much," she said as she guided him between her legs.

He lifted her thigh, hitching her leg around his hip, and sliding home. "Oh God." She gasped, dropping her head back, and rolling her eyes in pleasure.

"Don't ever forget, Julia. I can always do this to you," he said, in a hot whisper in her ear as he thrust into her.

"I know. I want it always."

"We have all of Manhattan for fucking. We have restaurants and bars, and theaters and museums, and I'm going to want to take you everywhere."

"No pun intended," she said, in between sexy little moans and pants.

"Take you *and* take you," he added. "Fuck you and make love to you. I'm not going to hold back. I'm going to seduce you all over this city, and make you come every single day and night."

"Please do," she said, her voice rising higher, her breath coming faster.

"All the time," he said, gripping her thigh harder, driving deeper. She responded by running her hands up his spine, and digging her fingernails deep into his skin.

"Leave marks on me," he told her, and she dug in harder. "I want scratch marks from you."

"You feel so fucking good, you're going to get them, Clay. Oh God, you're going to get them," she said, holding on tight and hard, dragging her nails along his muscles as she cried out, rocking her hips against his as she came, and soon, he chased her there with his own orgasm.

He wrapped his arms around her, needing to hold her, even in the stalled elevator. He layered kisses on her neck, already hot and sweaty. "Julia, I won't always take you hard like that, but sometimes I'm going to have to," he whispered.

"You better take me hard, and you better take me slow, and you better make love to me all night long," she said, pulling back to look him in the eyes. Hers were both fierce, and full of love.

"That's a promise, and I keep my promises to you," he said, running his thumb along her cheek.

"I know you do. That's why I'm here to stay."

That's where he always wanted her.

EPILOGUE

Two Months Later

"What can I get for you?"

The pair of young women in slouchy tops revealing bare shoulders had parked themselves in the burgundy bar stools at Speakeasy, where Julia was now a part-owner. They perused the cocktail menu, and then the blonde one lifted her face to Julia, the look in her eyes full of excitement. "Can you make the Purple Snow Globe? We heard this is the only bar where we can get it made fresh," she said, emphasizing that last word like it was made of sweet sugar. "I served some at a party last week from the store and everyone loved it, but we wanted to try the real thing."

"And I will be delighted to make it for you. But I should let you know, this isn't the only bar. There's a little place in San Francisco called Cubic Z that also makes a Purple Snow Globe, so if you ever find yourself out west, you know where to go," she said, and started mixing.

"Our friends are going to be so jealous. Everyone is loving this drink," the woman said.

"I'm thrilled to hear that."

After she set down the drinks, she headed to the back of the bar to retrieve more napkins. Along the way, her phone buzzed in her pocket, so she grabbed it. There was a text from Kim.

How's business? Booming as always, like it is here?

Julia tapped out an answer. *Always.* She dropped her phone back into her pocket, glad that Craig had taken over behind the bar for her. She still owned a stake in Cubic Z, but Craig had needed a job, and her move had given him the perfect chance to help his wife while she was busy with the newborn. Charlie hadn't been heard from, and while Julia and Clay had toyed with spreading a nasty rumor on Yelp about Charlie's chicken, they'd decided not to. Charlie was a man not to be messed with, so they'd chosen to leave him and his chicken in the past. But Julia couldn't deny she was pleased when her sister forwarded along a few new online reviews for Mr. Pong's that all noted the restaurant was less popular at lunch these days. Seemed that Charlie had lost a good portion of his venture capital patrons at the restaurant. Hunter with the laughing tell might have been kicked out of the poker circuit, but had managed the last word after all, telling his friends to find a new haunt for their kung pao chicken hankerings, hitting Charlie where it hurt him most.

As for her apartment, McKenna had packed up everything for her, deciding what needed to stay and what needed to go. She trusted her sister completely with that choice, especially when the boxes had arrived with only her favorite items in them. She didn't need her fluffy towels, though. Because she and Clay had bought new ones, with some of the $10,000 she'd won at the poker game, along with a bench, some softer pillows, and a new set of scarves. They'd considered ropes but they'd always been more DIY when it came to restraints, opting for belts, ties, panties and whatever was on hand, and that was likely to continue.

She pictured returning home tonight after her shift behind the bar. She'd find him naked in bed, sound asleep on his stomach, his strong back on display with the sheets low around his hips. The lights would be dim, the only sound the faint rhythm of his sleeping breath. She'd strip down to nothing, and run her hands along his skin. He'd groan lightly, roll over and pull her on top of him, and they'd have slow, sleepy, middle-of-the-night sex.

That image was burned in her brain as she returned to the bar to serve a new customer. A man in a suit had just sat down. Then she realized that man was her man. Her man in a suit, and by God, did he ever look sexy as hell in it. Maybe it was the little bit of cuff showing, or the cufflinks, or the purple tie he wore.

She rested her elbows on the bar, and flashed him a smile. "What can I get for you there, wearing your lucky tie?"

He ran his fingers down the fabric, and raised an eyebrow. "You noticed my lucky tie."

"I always notice what you're wearing," she said in a whisper, her words just for him. "Are you thinking you're getting lucky tonight?"

"I'm a lucky man every night because I have you."

"Flattery will get you everywhere. But you still must pay for your drink," she said and poured him his standard scotch, placing it in front of him. He took a long swallow, then reached for her hand, threading her fingers through his.

"Hey, gorgeous," he said softly.

"Hey, handsome."

"What would you think about going to Vegas this weekend?"

"So we can see your brother's show, then play a little blackjack?"

"For starters," he said, and there was a twinkle in his brown eyes.

A ribbon of possibility unfurled in her. "Are you going to propose to me in Vegas?"

He laughed. "Wouldn't you like to know?"

"I would like to know," she said, as the corners of her lips curved up.

"But I love surprises, Julia. So I guess you'll have to wait and see if I propose, or if maybe I take you there to elope."

She clasped his hand tighter, her way of saying she liked that idea. Either one. Both. "So I won't know till you take me to Vegas?"

He shrugged playfully. "Maybe I'll do neither. But I'll tell you this much. We will have an excellent time, and I fully intend on marrying you someday. Someday soon."

"Oh you do, do you?"

"I do."

"You practicing saying those words?" she said, teasing him like she'd always loved to.

"Maybe I am. Do you like hearing them from me?" he said, and every day she found new ways to fall in love with him. This was today's.

"I do, Clay. I do."

THE END

Check out my contemporary romance novels!

Caught Up In Us, a New York Times and
USA Today Bestseller! (Kat and Bryan's romance!)

Pretending He's Mine, a Barnes & Noble and
iBooks Bestseller! (Reeve & Sutton's romance)

Trophy Husband, a New York Times and
USA Today Bestseller! (Chris & McKenna's romance)

Playing With Her Heart, a
USA Today Bestseller! (Davis and Jill's romance)

Far Too Tempting, an Amazon romance
bestseller! (Matthew and Jane's romance)

And my USA Today Bestselling
No Regrets series that includes

The Thrill of It
(Meet Harley and Trey)

and its sequel

Every Second With You!

Stay tuned for NIGHTS WITH HIM, the next novel in the erotic romance Seductive Nights series, starring Michele Milo and her lover, slated for a fall 2014 release...

Ten years.

She'd been in love with one man for ten years.

That was far too long for a person to suffer through unrequitedness. But when would these feelings end? The guy she was seeing, Liam, was charming, and she'd hoped he'd blunt her love for the man she couldn't have. But as she flipped open her laptop to check on her next appointment, Michele wasn't sure if the spark was there with Liam – a true light-up-the-night ignition that could erase the past.

But it would take a once-in-a-century eclipse to blot out the ache she'd felt for that man who was now so happy with another woman.

Someday, she hoped she'd know freedom from this hurt in her heart, the way her whole chest wanted to cave in.

She clicked open her calendar, checking on the details of her next session. At least she had her work to focus on. Her patients and their challenges fed her, made her whole in a way that only her work as a psychologist could do. She scanned her notes, though she knew very little about her next patient. That was par for the course. She rarely knew much in advance and her job was to get to know patients during their time together. The little she gleaned from the referral was he was in law enforcement, and needed to be cleared to return to work.

That was her role. To figure out if he should be back on the streets.

Well, let's see what we've got, she figured, and she was ready to forget her own personal woes for the next hour.

When she heard a knock at two o'clock sharp, she opened the door to her office, and all thoughts rushed out of her brain but one.

One word. Blaring like a neon sign.

Smoldering.

This man was smoldering.

ACKNOWLEDGMENTS

Thank you to so many amazing people who helped me with this book. I am indebted, as always, to Cara. She is my ground zero for Clay, with her passion and insistence. In fact, there are three ladies who are the foundation of this book's existence – Hetty, Kim and Cara are the reason the Seductive Nights series is in your hands. They believed in these characters and this story. Thank you. Endless thank yous.

My early beta readers are indispensable and helped make the story better. Huge hugs and gratitude to Tanya Farrell, Kim Bias, Crystal Perkins and Jaime Collins. Each offered keen feedback and suggestions that were vital. As always, Jen McCoy rooted me on and assisted whenever I needed insight into particular areas. Wink, wink.

Sarah Hansen designed a gorgeous cover. Ali Smith took a fantastic photo. Helen Williams makes amazing graphics. Jesse can format the heck out of a book. Kelley keeps the ship running. Dawn Robinson lent her eagle eye to the final draft. Lauren McKellar helped make the words shine. Michelle navigates the crazy.

And my publicist, Kelly Simmon, is the best strategist there is. Tara Simone continues to guide me with her business wisdom, and my writer friends are my core group of support every day – Melody, Kendall, Violet, Monica, Jessie, Lexi and Sawyer.

Special shout outs to: Kristen Guay, Kathy Quates-Gilliam, Olayinka Adeniyi-Bello, Теодора Кузманова, and Maria Poli.

Thank you to early readers like Lara, Tiffany, Tiffany, Jennifer, Jamie, Reneall and Ginny for loving Clay.

Big thanks and love to many amazing supporters including: Lexi from Book Reviews by Lexi, Jennifer Santoro, Darcey Smith, Kelley, Kristyn and Tracey from Smut Book Junkie Book Reviews, Jennifer Marr, Kenna Nauenburg, MJ Fryer, Tanya at After the Final Chapters, Jennifer from Jen's Book Reviews, Tabby at Insightful Minds, Kristy Louise, Kara and Sandra from Two Book Pushers, Hetty from BestSellers & BestStellars, Jacquie Lamica, Tee From Kaidans Seduction, Yvette and Michelle from Nose Stuck in a Book, Vanessa Foxford, Valencia from Trulee V's Spot, Kim Bias, Sara Howe, Brenda Howe, Retta Rusaw at Because I Said So, Patricia Lee from A Literary Perusal, Theresa Potter, Stacy Hahn, Jassie DC, Julie Jules, Gretchen from About That Story, Tori and Kat and

Michelle and Mara from Give Me Books, Karen at The Danish Bookaholic, Crystal Perkins, Betsy from Book Drunk Blog, Tami Jo Schafer , Jennifer's Taking a Break, Simply Kristen, Helen from All Booked Out, Tink Bell, and Jaime Collins at For the Love of Books by Jaime, Two Crazy Girls With a Passion for Books, Lyndsey Aaron at The Eyeliner Manifesto, Angelica Maria Quintero, Georgette Geras-Waters Georgette from G & Co Book Blog, Kanae Eddings at Pearls and Peacocks, Wendy Racine, Kayla Eklund from Kayla's Reads and Reviews, Julie Jules Nichols, Carolyn Isherwood, Geri Slavinsky, Jessica Adkins from Bottles & Books Reviews, and Marianna from A Lust for Reading.

Last but not least, thank you to my loving family. They are my everything and I love them madly. Along with my dogs!!

CONTACT

I love hearing from readers! You can find me on Twitter at twitter.com/laurenblakely3, or Facebook at facebook.com/LaurenBlakelyBooks, or online at LaurenBlakely.com. You can also email me at laurenblakelybooks@gmail.com.

CPSIA information can be obtained at www.ICGtesting.com
Printed in the USA
BVOW09s2002061114

374010BV00017B/542/P